From the author

Writing has been an almost life-long hobby and interest for me that I have researched and developed over the years. I'm a big movie fan, which has inspired me to create my own worlds, characters and situations. I have only occasionally shared my interest with others, as I always felt it was very personal to me. However, of the friends & family who I have discussed my writing with, they have all encouraged me to take it further. So I would like to thank all those that have taken an interest and advised me.

I would especially like to thank my Dad. This book is dedicated to you, Pops.

A special note about this version

After some reflection and feedback, it was decided
to re-publish an updated version of this novel.
Therefore, this revised edition features material
which was not present in the original publication.

DYING GAMES SAGA

Book 1

CRAIG MICKLEWRIGHT

Showdown in Los Angeles

PROLOGUE

The cold rough of the pavement bit into her cheek, and the weight bearing down made it difficult for her to breathe. She eased open her eyes as a warm breeze made her hair dance, and looked to the window of the drugstore, fragments of glass littering the street. Cameron Willis was in big trouble. It had seemed an easy way out, such a simple job, not too risky. Little did she realise how loose the term 'friendship' meant to those who had been with her, and when the shit rained down … where were they now? Hiding and watching from the shadows, or long gone? Cameron suspected the latter.

The cop holding her down slowly relaxed his knee from the small of her back. If he had pressed any harder, she was sure he would have snapped her spine.

"Come on sister, you're going downtown." his rough, tobacco-coated voice announced, then she was lifted swiftly from the forecourt, bits of dirt and tarmac clinging to her face.

She gritted her teeth, his hold on her painful, and felt her sneaker-clad feet drag the ground. She was moved to the awaiting squad car, it's flashing light, accentuated by the night, sending a blue tint bouncing off every building.

In the back of the squad car, Cameron looked out of the window as she slumped awkwardly, the open door to the drugstore swinging in the breeze, a broken wire-mesh window hanging loose where Stacy had taken a crowbar to it. She remembered entering and treading on a packet of Paracetamol that must have fallen from a display stand. She had been nervous for sure, but an adrenaline seemed just shy of making itself known – that was until the alarm was tripped. Stacy, Gemma, Francesca and herself had only been there a moment when the lights came on, the same light that was now burning out of the front window and igniting the street.

A large female cop was interviewing the store owner who had been sleeping upstairs. Old man Barnaby. Cameron didn't feel any remorse. His insurance would surely cover the damage. One question just lingered in her head: what was she going to do now? The drugstore had been her only hope.

*

Soon she was thrown onto a chair in a small claustrophobic interview room, her hands still cuffed behind her back. *For Christ's sake*, she thought, *she was just a girl, what danger was she to anyone?* The large female cop guarded a door about two metres ahead beyond a desk, and directly in front sat a middle-aged detective, his face a tapestry of bumps and grazes, likely the result of a childhood acne problem, tired eyes lacking enthusiasm. He rubbed them with his finger and thumb before opening a file on the desk. Cameron's eyes remained fixed on him.

"Cameron Willis." He exhaled rhetorically.

She returned her best poker-face.

"You do realise that I'm only doing this because of your family and who your father happens to be, sweetheart. Otherwise, a petty B & E such as this wouldn't even get me out of bed."

The name tag pinned to his shirt read: 'Detective Inspector Jack Travern'.

"What were you doing at the Barnaby's drugstore, Cameron?"

"Er... I forgot to collect my prescription, detective?" Cameron eventually answered with that sarcastic attitude which had for too long been 'her thing'.

Travern slapped the file shut, staring at Cameron sternly, greying eyebrows pointing towards his nose.

"I'm guessing you're not stupid, Cameron, so I'll cut to the quick. You're looking at possibly a sentence for this. Your bag, it had a heavy stash of hard prescription medication and on the black market they are known to fetch big bucks. So you tell me who you were trying to steal this shit for, and maybe we can work something out that don't result in you spending the next few years in a jail cell."

Cameron just smirked, gently tugging at her cuffs, her arms starting to ache.

"Just give me my fuckin' phone call." - she said gruffly.

Travern looked incensed. He then abruptly got up, the chair falling to the floor with a crash, and he stormed off, opening the door. He then paused, glancing back to Cameron with venom.

"A smart-ass just like your big sister. We'll have her sitting in that chair again too, before long ... mark my words." He said, then walked out, slamming the door behind him which made the female Cop jolt as Cameron lowered her head with a sigh.

CHAPTER 1

Several weeks later…

Lowering her cell phone, she looked at the screen, where the display read 'call ended'. Thoughts lingered in her head of the conversation that had just played out. She was stuck, and any way out of the situation she found herself in, seemed hopeless. Yet she couldn't deny the feelings she still felt, and the woman that she still loved, regardless how the pain of the past had affected her. Cameron Willis sat cross legged on her bed, and placed her cell in a well-worn satchel, then fastened it shut. She got up from the bed and glanced around her room; a safe haven all her life, 23 years having flown by, changing and shaping her along the way. Posters of rock bands and horror movies adorned the walls, an iMac on a desk and a heap of makeup lying untidy on a dressing table. She sighed, wishing circumstances had turned out differently.

Leaving her room, she was greeted by the sight of her elder sister Patricia hobbling along the upstairs hallway towards her.

"Going somewhere?" Patricia then asked, supporting herself on steel crutches.

"I've got work. Life don't go on hold just 'cause you're home." Cameron retorted defensively.

"Oh, I forgot - you've still got that community work - how's it going?"

They met up at the top of a staircase that led down into a large open-plan foyer of the family home. Patricia was wearing a patterned, bright yellow sports bra, and loose-fitting shorts that revealed some bandaging around her left foot and ankle. Cameron had dressed in one of several tracksuits she owned, completing the look with an 'Angels' baseball cap that all but disguised a platinum blonde dye job. Her gold-plated lip-ring glinted in the glow of daylight.

"I suppose it's alright - beats sweeping the streets." Cameron added, turning to descend the steps.

"Yeah, you were lucky. If Dad hadn't pulled some strings for you... Hey, wait up! You gotta go straight out? You had any breakfast?"

Cameron sighed, "I'll get something on the way - I have to be there by eight."

Patricia glanced to a clock on the wall between the doors of two rooms. It was just gone seven.

"OK, you best hurry then. See you later, yeah?"

Cameron stared at her, the resemblance to one another not at first evident, Cameron being a bit of a Tom-boy, whilst Patricia was more feminine.

"You still thinking of moving on?" She asked with a hint of concern.

"I've been here for a while. But this ankle ain't letting me take the idea of going it alone all that seriously just yet. Why you askin', not trying to get rid of me, are you?" Patricia replied.

"Don't be stupid. It's just been, you know, nice having you home."

Patricia smiled, and touched her younger sister's arm, "No. I won't be going anywhere for a while. Got a few things to catch up on, if you know what I mean."

Cameron smiled back, then turned and hurried down the staircase. Patricia watched her go, remaining still for a second, relieved that things were finally getting better between the two of them after their history. She then proceeded after her, physically unable to rush. But life was not a series of rules and regulations anymore. She could now look forward to a brand-new beginning. Yet before she could contemplate any of that, she needed to find and speak to her brother Malcolm.

*

Meanwhile on a stretch of road leading towards Downtown LA, a red Lotus Esprit travelled, with Malcolm - Patricia & Cameron's playboy brother at the wheel. He spoke hands-free on the phone as a bright, morning sunshine burned through the windscreen.

"Well, I've just got a contact of mine to meet with, babe, then we'll have breakfast. I was thinking that Italian joint, Satrarelli's in Santa Monica?" He said.

"That sounds great. What time should I expect you?" the voice of his fiancé asked through the phone.

Malcolm glanced to a gleaming, expensive-looking Rolex as he gripped the wheel, and his own face reflected back; cleanly shaven, sporting subtle side burns and spiked, dark-brown hair. He then turned down another street, and headed for the suburbs.

"About ten I'd say. I shouldn't be much longer than that."

"Alright, Malcolm - I'll just finish my Cheerios and then start getting ready."

Malcolm ended the call then eased his foot off the accelerator. The Lotus then pulled into an underground car park belonging to a high-rise apartment building, the brightness of the morning quickly sinking into darkness.

Parking beside a gun-metal grey 4X4 Jeep, Malcolm extinguished the engine, before rolling the window down on his door.

"Little late, aren't we, Mr Willis?" came a throaty voice, then the jeep's window came down to reveal a large, muscular Black guy at the wheel. A smaller, bare-chested man of similar ethnic descent sat with him, listening obliviously to a concealed iPod.

"Has your boss thought about my proposition?" Malcolm asked.

"You must realise, Mr Willis, my employer has investors in his clubs from all over the world - please explain what the fuck makes you so special?" the muscular Black man asked.

"I bring more than just a number to the deal. I have a lot of influence amongst a lot of people. What I bring to this could be highly beneficial to everyone concerned."

The man sighed, then revealed a phone, and pressed a button. Malcolm listened carefully.

"Hey, Boss - yeah, I'm with him now. He seems ok - what you want me to give him?"

A brief silence came and went, and Malcolm guessed the man's employer was detailing orders. He checked his Rolex again.

"OK, Boss - I'll tell him, but, I dunno - maybe he won't be interested."

Malcolm and the man looked at each other and

Malcolm wished he could hear what was being said on the other end of the phone.

The call then ended and the man put the cell away, suddenly climbing out of the jeep, revealing just how big he was; the belt buckle on his waist reaching the roof of the Lotus. Malcolm climbed out also, following the man-mountain to the back of the jeep, and glanced to the smaller man as he went - who was still consumed by his 'tunes.

"What'd he say?" Malcolm enquired, patience waning.

"My employer doesn't go into these things lightly - he knows that whoever he works with has gotta be trustworthy."

"Just quit stalling, buddy and tell me what he said."

The man turned to look at him sternly, before glancing around to check they were still alone in the echoey, baron car park.

"OK man, here's the 4-1-1. He tells me you need to do one thing for him. He requires information from some dude called 'Gerard Jones'. Thing is though, there's a problem. This guy did a job for him, and stashed a whole heap o' cash somewhere. The only thing is, the law screwed this Gerard guy over some old charges, and he's currently doing work at a drop-in centre."

Malcolm suddenly felt concerned.

"The boss wants you to find this Gerard Jones dude, and get him to talk. We can't touch him, but the boss knows that you can."

"How does he?" Malcolm retorted.

"Because he has word that your little sister is currently doing the same thing. She probably rubs shoulders with the dude every day. Get her to talk to him and nail the information before midnight tonight ... then my employer will meet with you."

Malcolm turned away, suddenly feeling uneasy, "Hey, I dunno, I didn't want my family involved - you sure there's no other way?"

"Do this thing 'cuz - and you never know, you might one day become a real player in this town."

Malcolm sighed, then walked back to the Lotus.

"I'll be in touch." He replied, then climbed in and fired up the engine.

* *

Just over an hour later, the telephone rang in the foyer of the family's Bel-Air based mansion. Their mother Barbara, an Attorney for over twenty years, lifted the handset.

"Willis residence..." She announced,

"Oh, Mrs Willis? It's Jeanie - don't suppose Malcolm's there, is he?"

Barbara instantly recognised the voice of her son's fiancée. She liked 'Jeanie', a good-natured girl, and definitely more respectable than some of the girls Malcolm was known to have associated with in his youth. They were engaged to be married - but alas, any date was yet to be set.

"Erm, no Jeanie - I haven't seen him since last night - why?" She replied.

"Oh it's nothing, just that he called me this morning, saying he had some business to take care of, and we'd go for breakfast around ten."

Barbara glanced to an antique, likely priceless grandfather clock by the staircase. It had just turned half past ten. She understood why Jeanie had phoned. If anything, Malcolm was usually a good time keeper.

"Maybe he's been delayed. Have you tried his cell?" She replied.

"Yes, but it's switched off - all I'm getting is Jack Nicholson on his voice mail - but you'd think he'd phone to say if he was going to be late."

"Well, Malcolm can't rightly do that if you're talking to me, can he now?"

She heard Jeanie sigh.

"Of course, yes. I'll speak to you again. Thanks Mrs Willis." Jeanie replied, then abruptly hung up, and Barbara lowered the handset before focusing on a framed picture on the wall near the door; a family portrait featuring herself, her husband Edward, and their three children - Malcolm, Patricia & Cameron. It had been taken some years ago when they were on vacation in the south of France. The picture seemed to reflect a close and loving family - which seemed in stark contrast to the present. With a heavy heart, Barbara turned away, returning the handset to its charging cradle.

"Who was that, mom?" a voice called from another room.

Barbara walked into the living room which led into the kitchen and saw Patricia propped up on a stool beside a marble work surface, finishing a bowl of frosted flakes.

"Was that Malcolm?" Patricia asked.

"No, it was Jeanie. She was asking after your brother." Barbara replied.

The sun that beamed in from the kitchen window lit them both up, and their facial features and long fair hair were strikingly similar. Barbara had worked in law for many years, and was just shy of 62, but had retained a noticeable portion of her youth. Patricia, a former University graduate with a past where she had worked as a Private Eye, had not long turned 28, and was the picture of her mother when she had been that age.

"What made her call here? She knows he never stays over. He and James went onto a club if I recall. Didn't he go back to the hotel after that?" She asked.

"Well, he called Jeanie, so I'm guessing not. He was going to take her for breakfast apparently, but hasn't shown up."

"Has she tried to his cell?"

"It's switched off, so I suggested she wait to hear off him. I'm sure there's a reasonable explanation."

Patricia took a mouthful of flakes and munched loudly as her mother prepared coffee. The strong smell of the family-favoured brand began to fill the room.

"Want one?" She asked.

Patricia shook her head as she licked some sugar from her lips.

CHAPTER 2

Malcolm's Lotus was parked across the road from a four-story building that only a year previous had been converted into a Youth Hostel. A few kids had been kicking a ball back and forth a short distance ahead, but stopped their game on noticing the sleek sports car. From Malcolm's vantage point he could see into the rear courtyard of the building, and observed a few older youths playing basketball, whilst others sat or stood around talking. He then opened the glove compartment, taking out a pair of binoculars, and raised them to his eyes.

After a moment, he spotted his youngest sister in a room on the second floor, folding what looked like bed sheets and tidying them away inside a cupboard. He watched her working for a few more seconds, before eventually raising a cell phone to his ear, then watched as she reacted to his call.

"Malcolm?" came her voice.

"Cameron?" He replied, "Hey sis - can we talk? I'm

outside in the Lotus."

"What? Why Malcolm? I'm under a pretty strict regime - you so much as talk back to some of the people here and they note it down for their weekly reports."

"It's important - I wouldn't ask you if it wasn't - now just make an excuse and come down to the street and talk to me. And make it snappy."

Malcolm noticed how Cameron was reluctant to comply - but he *had to get her alone*, if only to test the ground.

"OK, I'll think of something." She agreed.

He watched her end the call and conceal the cell in her tracksuit pocket, before turning away. She was then stopped in her tracks by a guy of similar age dressed smartly in a black shirt, unshaven and with black slicked-back hair. *Who's the poser*, Malcolm wondered.

Inside the large office-come-storage room, Cameron stared at the youth with concern.

"Gerard?? W-what are you doing here?"

"Small world, ain't it, sweet 'art?" the youth replied in a strong East London accent, before lighting up a cigarette.

He offered the packet of Molboro Menthols to Cameron, and she unsheathed one, stepping away from the window, and thus out of Malcolm's viewpoint.

After a brief pause, she said "What they get you on? I hope you know I never said nothing."

"Relax darling, its fine - it was an old rap - circumstantial horses-shit, but enough to get me two months workin' 'ere." Gerard replied, and offered his lighter to Cameron, igniting the tip of the cigarette as she placed it between her thick, full lips.

Cameron took a long drag, then exhaled a thick cloud of smoke, before focusing on Gerard again, eyeing him up and down sheepishly.

"Come here, darlin'." He said, then embraced her, squeezing her tight.

"Erm, I er..." Cameron stammered, separating, "I've gotta go out for a minute, my brother's just called, and wants a word." She said, then rushed out. Just the simplest touch from Gerard suddenly made her stomach tie itself in knots.

Gerard had noticed how easily she had turned red, and he frowned, picking up on her nervous disposition.

"Your brother huh? Well don't be too long; we got a lot to discuss you and I." He said, and watched her hurry out of the room like she couldn't wait to get away.

A couple of minutes later, Malcolm jolted to a rap of knuckles on his window, and he sat up, having nearly dozed off, and rolled the window down.

Cameron peered in at him, hair fluttering beneath her baseball cap from the morning breeze.

"Make this quick, Malcolm. What's this about?" She asked, exhaling smoke, then let the cigarette fall, treading it out with her foot.

Malcolm stared at her, "Get in, we've gotta go for a drive." He replied.

Confused, Cameron walked around to the other side and climbed in, whilst at the same time, up in the second-floor window, Gerard was watching, and followed the Lotus with his eyes as it pulled away from the kerb, then sped off down the road.

"Why all the cloak and dagger shit? Is it Patricia again? Is she in trouble?" Cameron asked.

"No, it's nothing to do with your sister - and I don't want you saying anything about this to her, do I make myself clear?"

"Yeah sure … jeez. So, you gonna tell me what's crawled up your ass then? And I can't be gone long, or I'll be in trouble myself."

Malcolm sighed, realising he had to get straight to the point, "Do you know a guy going by the name of 'Gerard Jones'?" He asked sternly.

Cameron's heart skipped a beat, "Excuse me, er...who?" She replied.

"Gerard Jones - goofy fuckin' name if you ask me. I have reason to believe he's working at the same place you are. Have you seen him yet, or spoken to him even?"

"There's a few guys working there, but well, it's not really the kinda place for casual introductions. Why do you ask?"

Cameron purposely avoided eye-contact.

"It's nothing."

"Hey come on Malcolm, you obviously want to know for a reason."

Malcolm brought the Lotus to a halt in a side street, leaving the finely tuned engine purring.

"Well, it's like this. There's a guy I'm planning to go into business with, and before we make any deal, he wants me to get some information out of this Jones character. Now, if it's suspect, which it likely will be, then it wouldn't look good someone of my stature meeting with him - but you're working with him." Malcolm explained.

"Hey hang on - who's this guy you're going into business with, and what's he want?" Cameron retorted.

"I can't say. just tell him to call this number..." - Malcolm took a pen out of his suit jacket along with a business card, then scribbled a number on the back.

"...at seven tonight - no later than that - I'd prefer to keep you as much in the dark about this as possible - for all I know, this Jones guy could owe my contact big time, and I wouldn't like you anywhere near if things were to go bad."

Cameron took the card and looked at the number.

"Where's this then?" She asked.

"Better you don't know angel face. Now put it away, and I'll drop you back." Malcolm replied, then adjusted the gears and reversed back onto the main road, hand-breaking the Lotus around to face the way they had come, then accelerated with a screech of tires.

*

As evening drew in, and the sun began to dip over the horizon, a Taxi Cab arrived outside a partly-abandoned apartment building. Cameron climbed out and paid the Mexican-looking driver before hurrying up the litter-strewn steps in front of the tall building. A gentle pitter-patter of rain had begun to fall, and Cameron felt vulnerable in just her track suit, the day having started out so warm. She began to regret not bringing an overcoat as she rang the bell.

Minutes later, on the third floor, Cameron came out of an old elevator, rolling back an iron gate and was met with a corridor covered in graffiti, and rubbish littered the floor all around. She held her satchel over her shoulder, and walked on, until she eventually reached an apartment door. The building's resident stray cat sat crying. Cameron reached down and petted it, before pounding on the door twice with a clenched fist. After a few seconds, it opened to reveal a woman a few years her senior, with long brown hair, and a rather scary-looking complexion.

"Cameron? Shit, I thought it was my landlord again." She said, then opened the door wide, allowing Cameron entry as the cat ran away.

As the woman closed and instinctively bolted the door, Cameron looked around, then wrinkled her nose up at the strong, unpleasant smell in the air, like unwashed laundry and a lack of hygiene.

"So, you're finally more than just a voice at the end of a phone. I haven't seen you in weeks." the woman remarked, eyes exploring Cameron's presence from head to toe as she herself stood there in a loose-fitting grey sweater, torn joggers and socks.

Cameron returned a reluctant smile. Her friend had certainly seen better days. She guessed her hair hadn't been washed for some time, and it was quickly becoming obvious who the source of the odour was.

"Davina, I er … I wanted to come, but like I said this morning, things have been pretty fucked up for me these last few weeks. I didn't want to come over unless I could bring you something." Cameron replied.

Davina glanced to her friend's satchel optimistically.

"So, h-have you scored me some stuff?" She asked, reaching a hand out.

Cameron immediately noticed the track marks that discoloured her arms, and she backed off.

"Hey, what the fuck!? Looks like somebody's done more than alright since the last time we saw each other." She commented with disapproval, and Davina quickly lowered her rolled up sleeves, letting the ends hang loosely over her knuckles.

She smirked, revealing discoloured teeth, "What can I say - I wasn't gonna wait around for however many weeks just for you. A guy in apartment 12B fixed me up. But I've ran out now. What you brought me?" She asked, looking pitiful.

"I haven't brought a thing, Davina. I'm lying pretty low myself right now."

Davina's expression changed, "What do you mean? Are you in trouble?"

"I couldn't handle things the way they were. It was driving me fuckin' crazy. So me and some friends tried to turn over a pharmacy, but ... it didn't work out."

Davina was impressed, "What happened?"

"My so-called girlfriends dumped me as soon as the alarm went off, and before I knew what was happening, I was face down on the ground, having my hands cuffed behind my back." Cameron explained with some unease at the memory.

"Shit." Davina remarked, then walked into the

living room, where a moth-eaten sofa was dressed up in blankets, showing that she hadn't even been up to going to bed at night.

Mugs of half-drunk coffee littered the table in the middle of the room, and a tinfoil ashtray was on the floor beside the sofa, overflowing with cigarette butts. Cameron felt a mixture of pity and disgust.

"So, what they land you with?" Davina asked.

"Just community work, at a hostel - thank God." Cameron replied.

"I suppose it could have been worse - you could have been sweeping the streets and picking up dog shit."

"Or facing time. Yeah I know, I was real lucky."

Davina sat down on her sofa-come-bed, and picked up the ashtray, stubbing yet another cigarette into it. A few butts fell to the floor.

"So, you not brought anything, nothing at all? Not even a few pills?" She asked.

Cameron sat down reluctantly in an armchair where a pair of dirty knickers were draped across the arm.

"Sorry, no, but I had to see you. I've got some news." She said.

"What like?"

"I might be able to score you some stuff in a day or two. You see, Gerard Jones is back in town, and I think he's still interested in me, in-fact, I'm more than sure he is."

"Gerard Jones? I thought you said you couldn't handle things the way they were - he isn't someone you can just hop in and out of bed with - he has to feel like he owns you before he gives up the skag, and that's what you couldn't handle, isn't it?"

"Well, there was more to it than that - but, I dunno, he seemed different when I spoke with him this morning, he was dressed better, despite being on some charge and doing the same community work at the same place I am." Cameron confessed.

"Ooh, cozy."

"Well, anyway I haven't asked him yet, but he was kind of hands-on when we were alone together, so I can't see a problem with us returning to the old arrangement."

Davina bowed her head, "Well, just come up with something soon, Cameron. The stuff the clinic gives me does nothing. The damn cramps are as bad as ever, and I can't sleep at night no more." She stared at her friend, eyes welling up "I'm having nightmares and the sweat at times is just dripping off me."

Cameron leaned forward, placing a hand on Davina's knee "I'll get you something; don't worry about that." She reassured, despite lacking the courage of her convictions.

CHAPTER 3

When Cameron met Davina

5 years ago…

It was an afternoon in early June as Cameron sat on a bench beside the outdoor basketball court at the college she'd attended on weekdays. Alexandra, better known as Alex; a girlfriend of about a year or so, had just scored a hoop much to the delight of her team. As the referee called the end of the first quarter, she then smiled as Alex jogged over, looking gorgeous in her tight-fitting kit, complete with knee socks and ginger hair tied in pigtails. Cameron hadn't really been one at that stage for public displays of affection, but as she stood up to greet Alex, they flung their arms around each other, and Alex kissed her full on the lips.

Cameron was wearing the same black & white kit as the rest of her team, with the other team's colours being a pale blue. It wasn't a big game or anything, just for fun really - but regardless the middle-aged female referee always took it very seriously. Cameron glanced around to see if anyone was watching, but most of her class mates were quite open-minded, and a gay relationship was nothing unusual. It was then that she looked beyond the basketball court, through the wire mesh railings and noticed three girls hanging out by the stands - one was looking right back at them, especially focusing on Cameron.

Davina was one of three girls who had been caught more than a few times smoking or drinking on the campus grounds. They were not from the college itself but from a run-down neighbourhood that was located nearby. Davina had noticed Cameron a few times and going by how her and Alex acted, quickly guessed she was gay. On this occasion she was taken by Alex's kiss and Cameron's obvious embarrassment - showing signs that 'out' wasn't all that 'out' for Cameron, which made her instantly alluring.

"Just go and talk to her, Davina." one of her friends piped up, and Davina approached the railings as she saw Alex hurry out of the court at the far end, and Cameron returned Davina's stare and decided to approach. They met up either side of the railings and Davina's eyes explored Cameron's face.

"Your friend's good at the game, huh?" Davina

remarked, as Cameron glanced to the watching girls a few feet behind the dark-haired grunge outcast.

"Oh... it was a lucky shot." She answered.

"Do they ever let you play?"

"Not lately, not since I punched a girl in the face for tackling Alex last semester."

Davina chuckled.

"I'm sure she deserved it ... I wish I'd seen that."

Cameron sniggered, blushing slightly, "She cried like a little baby."

Cameron's hand gripped the railings and Davina came closer, reaching up to grab the railings also, and the two entwined fingers.

"Hey..." Davina lowered her voice, "When's your classes over?"

Cameron stared at her, then glanced back to the basketball court as a few girls started to return.

"I, er... 4:30." Cameron stammered, then backed off as Davina grinned.

"So maybe I'll catch ya later? I can usually be found by the gates. You might wanna come alone."

Cameron looked back and spotted Alex as she returned to the court with her team mates.

"I don't know. I'll think about it... I-I gotta go." She replied then hurried to join the others.

Cameron met up with Alex who looked over to

Davina just as she returned to the other two girls.

"Who was that?" she asked with confusion.

"Oh nobody … They were just trying to bum cigarettes." Cameron lied then grabbed Alex's hand as everyone returned to the game for the next quarter.

*

As evening drew in, Cameron, now in a simple T-shirt and Levi's wandered up to the tall, closed iron gates of the college. The sun was dipping over the hills and the wind had begun to pick up. Looking around she began to feel stupid. What was she thinking trying to meet up with this girl? What about Alex? She pictured her cute girlfriend's face for a moment and a deep feeling of regret engulfed her. She turned to walk away, then gasped as a horn sounded and she then saw an old, beaten-up camper van arrive.

The window then came down to reveal Davina, sporting a pair of round sunglasses.

"Hey kid. Jump in. I thought you weren't coming. Just as well I took another drive 'round the block. If we're quick we'll still make the six o'clock." She said.

Cameron took a moment to compose herself, then approached the van, "The six o'clock?" she enquired.

Davina grinned, "Yeah at the drive in. You'll never guess what they're showing. It's some anniversary special presentation."

"What they showin'?"

"Only 'Near Dark'!"

"Near... what?"

Davina chuckled, "Just get in … you're gonna love it. You like vampire movies, right?"

"I guess." Cameron answered then without further hesitation, found herself walking around to the passenger side and climbing in.

About an hour later, at the local drive in, one of the few remaining in L.A. Bill Paxton could be seen up on the big screen, just as he walked along the counter of a bar, much to the shock and terror of the bar tender the other side. He then suddenly kicked out, slicing the bar tender's throat with the spur on his boot, before jumping down behind the counter to feed.

Davina chuckled her enthusiasm at the horror on screen, and Cameron looked away, bemused. She checked her watch, and it was approaching seven thirty. She then raised her slushy from her lap, wrapped her lips around the straw and sucked.

Davina glanced to her then was surprised when Cameron reached for the door and opened it, quickly exiting the van. Davina went to grab her by the arm but wasn't quick enough.

Outside the van, Cameron walked away alongside a row of parked vehicles. Music and screams could still be heard coming from the movie, but she had lost interest. Her conscience had got the better of her and she now felt the quicker she was out of the situation the better. The drive-in was located in the hills, and as she walked out of the gates she was greeted with a view of the city, now starting to shimmer as night drew in.

"Cameron!" Davina shouted, hurrying after her, "Wait up... where you going?"

Cameron walked on, increasing her stride then turned onto the street ... just as a group of girls came walking towards her.

One of them was Alex, laughing and talking as she walked, until she stopped in her tracks on seeing Cameron.

Davina then appeared behind, much to Alex's surprise.

"Cameron? Thought you said you had to study? Er... what she doing here?" Alex responded at suddenly seeing Cameron and the mystery girl from earlier.

Cameron stood open-mouthed; slushy held to her chest. Davina then reached out and lay her hand on Cameron's shoulder, smiling at Alex.

"Alex!" Cameron replied, not knowing what to say.

Davina ran her hand from Cameron's shoulder

and down her arm affectionately. Alex looked incensed, then suddenly stepped forward to thrust her hand up to smash the slushy container all over Cameron's face and chest - red strawberry crushed-ice going everywhere.

Davina stumbled away to avoid the splash, and watched as Alex turned and ran away crying, her friends following after her, with one giving Cameron a disapproving look before leaving.

Davina then walked around to view Cameron from the front who was standing soaked and humiliated.

"Fuck." was all she could comment.

A few minutes later, a tearful Cameron was standing beside Davina's van now parked in the car park of the drive-in, engine running. Davina then rolled open the side door from within, and offered her hand to Cameron.

"Come on girl, jump in I've got a change of clothes back here. You can't go back looking like that."

Cameron looked at her, then took Davina's hand, and climbed inside. Sitting on her haunches with Davina, who rolled the van door shut again, she wiped a runny nose, then took her stained T-shirt off over her head. Davina turned and rummaged in a hold-all before pulling out a checked shirt. She turned to pass it to Cameron, who she thought looked vulnerable in just her bra and Levi's. Davina felt for her, even though she knew she was partly to blame. Before handing her the shirt, she reached a hand out to catch a tear as it escaped Cameron's left eye.

"Hey girl come here. Don't be cryin' now." She said tenderly and Cameron smiled, as Davina embraced her, holding her tight and comforting. Then after a moment, Cameron began to kiss Davina's neck, leading up to her ear which she nibbled.

"Er... What are you doing?" Davina whispered.

Cameron continued kissing her neck then breathed her response: "Making love to you."

The two girls then collapsed onto some make shift bedding and let their mutual attraction take over.

CHAPTER 4

"See? I said I'd make it up to you!" Malcolm announced to Jeanie as they stood in the reception of the Roosevelt Hotel getting on for seven in the evening.

"It'll take a bit more than money and wine to talk me around." Jeanie replied - she was a pretty, if slightly overweight woman in her early thirties with cropped mousy brown hair, dressed elegantly in a tight-fitting waist coat and trousers, perfume intoxicating.

Malcolm put his arm around her and squeezed her against him, "Hey, don't be like that - I said I was sorry, and anyway, I had a lot on." He explained, equally well dressed in a tailored three piece suit.

A snooty-looking waiter approached, holding a guest list pinned to a clip board.

"Mr & Mrs Willis?" He said, eyes jumping impatiently from Jeanie to Malcolm then back to the guest list.

Jeanie frowned, as Malcolm looked at the waiter

and smiled.

"That's us, pal - is our table ready?"

"Yes of course, sir – please, right this way." the waiter continued, turning on his heels.

Soon they were seated at a table in the centre of the restaurant area of the hotel, and Malcolm perused a wine list. Piano music played gently in the background. Jeanie stared at him and couldn't keep mad, always a sucker for her fiancé's flamboyant taste.

"It's nice here - what made you pick this place? I had been so psyched for Satrarelli's..." She asked looking around, and picked out a bread stick from a container, taking a bite.

"Well, those fancy restaurants up and down the street cater for a certain clientele, but even then, I felt you deserve better. You only eat here under strict reservation."

"And what about that Mr & Mrs thing? It had a nice ring to it … don't you think?"

"Well, there's an unspoken rule at places like this about unmarried couples - so as we're engaged anyway, I thought … what the hell."

Jeanie grinned her heightened enthusiasm. Just then, the same waiter came over, and whispered in Malcolm's ear, quickly turning Jeanie's enthusiasm into concern.

"What is it?" She asked as the waiter stepped back,

and Malcolm got up, looking troubled.

"I don't know, I'm wanted on the phone - shouldn't take a minute. Order for us, yeah babe? I'll have whatever you're having." He replied, then straightened his clothes and left.

Jeanie was bemused but not surprised, reaching over to a menu on a nearby table, and thumbed through the pages, letting a loud sigh escape her lips.

Malcolm reached a telephone in a narrow corridor near the kitchen, and lifted the receiver, whilst at the same time checking his Rolex.

"Gerard Jones I presume?" He said in a low voice.

In a well decorated apartment across town, Gerard stood in his living room by a drinks cabinet, wearing an open shirt and Levis, his black hair dripping wet, chest slick with perspiration.

"So, what do I call you then, Mr?" He replied.

"Malcolm Willis, I don't do pseudonyms. I'll get straight to it. This is about a mutual friend of ours, and he's asked me to do him a favour and get you and him to meet up."

Gerard smirked, "I guess you're in a public place, and it isn't exactly convenient to talk, would that be right?"

Malcolm stepped aside as a waiter came out of a kitchen pushing a trolley full of eye-catching desserts.

"Very astute of you, Mr Jones. Now I'm sure you know the score, so I'll telephone our friend with the news that you'll be at his club no later than 11:30 - do we have an understanding?" He added.

Gerard walked out of the living room carrying the cordless phone and glanced into a steam filled bathroom, where someone could be seen showering behind frosted glass.

"I'll be there." He replied, then lowered the phone, switching it off, and glanced into the bathroom again.

"Sweet cheeks?" He announced.

The figure behind the screen didn't reply, the noise of the running water clearly too loud. Gerard then grabbed a coat off a hook on the wall and hurried out, slamming the front door behind him. The shower went off in reaction.

"Gerard?" Cameron called, her face then peering out from behind the screen, water dripping from her hair and chin.

Minutes later Malcolm returned to Jeanie, who was looking more than a little disgruntled.

"Who was that? Can't we even go for a meal without your lowlife friends ringing you up??!" She remarked, speaking from experience.

"Sorry about that, babe. It was a business contact. Nothing for you to worry about. So ... did you order for us?"

Jeanie bowed her head and opened the menu before her, "You're having the Lobster. I ordered the special."

"What about the wine?" Malcolm added.

"They've got a lot of stuff written pretentiously in French. So, I told our waiter we'd order the wine when the meals arrive."

Malcolm nodded, noticing Jeanie's change in mood, and stuffed a napkin into his shirt collar.

"Is that entirely necessary?" Jeanie said giving him daggers.

"This suit was a thousand bucks. Can we just try and enjoy this? I don't want to get indigestion before I've even had a bite to eat." Malcolm replied, and grabbed the wine list.

(10:35pm)

A black van pulled up before a set of tall iron gates, and the headlights dipped. Gerard was at the wheel, and Jay-Z played quiet on the radio.

"Now, you understand, tonight wasn't just a one-time deal. This isn't over just because I cut you some slack this once." He said to Cameron, who didn't look at him as she opened her door, the cool night air suddenly so inviting.

"I'll expect you to make good on your promise tomorrow. Tell me you understand?" He added, grabbing her by her wrist, and she looked at him.

"Got it. Can I go now??" She answered, and Gerard loosened his grip, allowing her to climb out, and watched her as she let herself in through the gate, before hurrying up the long driveway to the Willis family Mansion.

Cameron entered through the front door to be met by a worried looking Patricia who was wearing pink silk pyjamas and supporting herself on a single crutch.

"I hope you know Mom and Dad have been going stir crazy. Where have you been until now??" She quizzed.

Cameron walked past her, approaching the staircase, "I met an old friend at lunch - we decided to go for a few drinks after I was done at the hostel. I would have called, but I kind of lost track of the time." She replied, then began to ascend the steps, looking and feeling exhausted.

Patricia watched her with concern, not really sure if she believed her kid sister, but also knew it didn't lead anywhere pressing her.

Eventually, Cameron entered her bedroom, kicking off her shoes and tossed her satchel and baseball cap onto the bed, before walking into the on-suite bathroom. When inside, she unzipped her tracksuit top, removing it slowly, then discarded it to reveal a thin, pale-red sleeveless vest, which had been put on inside-out. Turning to a mirror located above the wash basin, Cameron hooked her fingers into the hem of her vest, to quickly peal it off over her head. Then as she dropped it to the floor, now wearing little more than tracksuit bottoms and a black lace bra, she winced in pain at the deep red scratch marks disfiguring her left breast. She stepped closer to the mirror, leaning over the basin, and touched the scratches gently, which left traces of blood on her fingertips. She sighed, before running the taps, and splashing some refreshing water on her face.

Cameron returned to the bedroom a couple of minutes later, wearing a white dressing gown that matched her striking platinum blonde hair, and she slipped her feet into a pair of slippers before sitting down on the bed. She grabbed her satchel and opened the top, retrieving an empty lunch box and a water bottle. She placed them neatly on a small cupboard next to the bed, then upturned her satchel emptying the remainder of its contents onto the floor. Bending down, she routed through a host of cosmetics, a half-eaten candy bar and a wrist watch, before eventually picking up a padded manila envelope. Staring at it in silence, she then opened it carefully, and emptied its contents onto her lap. Then she just focused, her nerves playing hell with her as she lay eyes upon two unused needles and a little transparent sachet of brown powder.

Cameron walked into the living room minutes later on-route to the kitchen, where Patricia was preparing Cocoa as their father; high-court Judge Edward Willis, dozed in an armchair in front of the television.

"So, who's this friend?" Patricia asked, waiting for the kettle to boil.

"Oh, nobody you would have known." Cameron replied candidly, opening the refrigerator and taking out a bottle of orange juice.

"You sure you want that? I can do you a mug of cocoa if you prefer." Patricia offered.

Cameron shook her head, pouring the OJ into a glass, before returning it to the refrigerator and closing the door. Patricia heard the kettle click, and began to pour the steaming water into her prepared mug, then stirred the cocoa with a spoon. Cameron watched without her elder sister knowing, but turned away as soon as Patricia looked up.

"Is everything alright, sis?" Patricia asked.

Cameron sipped the OJ whilst looking at a photograph pinned to a notice board on the wall, of herself when she was in school, receiving an award for an art competition. The painting she had entered now hung pride of place in the living room, and from where she was standing, she could see it above the open log fireplace. It was a landscape picture of the small country cabin the family often went to during the school holidays.

"Cameron?" came her sister's voice again, "Is something wrong?"

"Why do you keep questioning me??!" Cameron suddenly snapped, turning to look at Patricia, "What's with all the questions? Why do you give such a damn anyway? Why the sudden concern?"

Her raised voice alerted their father, who jolted awake, all blurry eyed and confused. He sat up, then looked into the kitchen as Patricia backed off from Cameron.

"I was only asking! We were all worried about you." She retorted.

"That's rich, you worrying about me. Who are you to be worried about me?!" Cameron shouted.

"Hey!" Edward's voice then called, "Don't talk to your sister like that, Cameron - she's been through a lot lately."

Cameron looked into the living room at him.

"Oh she has, has she? Well, what about me? Ever thought about that, Dad? Things haven't exactly been rosy for me either - not that any of you would care to notice!" She replied, then stormed off, taking her OJ and returning upstairs.

Patricia & Edward were left looking at each another, flabbergasted.

(11:45pm)

Malcolm entered the foyer of Donnelly's Night Club getting on for midnight, and was met by a big, Black bouncer in a tuxedo.

"Oh, hello." Malcolm said, feeling a thump-thump-thump vibration in his toes, whilst eyeing up two scantily clad girls coming out of a bathroom, who giggled together as they passed by.

"Can I help you, sir?" the bouncer asked, doing his best intimidating stare.

Malcolm focused on him indifferently, then smiled, "That's a good question, pal, perhaps you could point me in the direction of your boss?"

The bouncer looked puzzled, "Your name … pal?" He retorted.

Malcolm produced a business card, quickly handing it to the bouncer, "Here, this is all the information you're going to need."

The bouncer looked at the card, sighing at Malcolm's cocky tone.

"OK, this way sir - apparently Mr Donnelly is expecting you."

"I didn't doubt it for a second." Malcolm added annoyingly, then followed whilst eyeing up the two girls as they stood in a doorway, loud thumping dance music spilling out from within.

Soon a knock came to the door of an office on the second floor, and Malcolm stood humming an incomprehensible tune beside the bouncer, until the door opened. They were met by the face of a young woman with cropped black hair and large brown, pixie-like eyes.

"Mr Donnelly's other guest has arrived, ma'am." the bouncer said.

The woman, who was probably in her late twenties, eyed Malcolm up and down, and in response he returned a confident smile, a sense of recognition to his eyes.

"Well come on in then, sir." She said, and opened the door to allow Malcolm entry, and he walked in, leaving the bouncer to wonder off back downstairs.

Inside the large, elegantly decorated office, Malcolm was led to a central desk, and he offered his hand out to a man of similar age to himself, who was seated in a high back leather chair. He had a shaven head, and as the two men shook hands, he revealed a set of gold capped teeth.

"Mr Willis - I take it you've already met my associate..." the man said, and Malcolm looked to a long leather bench by the wall the other side of the door, to see Gerard Jones reclining on it as the woman handed him a bottle of Budweiser.

"Thanks, Justine." Gerard said, and the woman, wearing tight black denim, smiled before walking back to their host and standing trophy-like beside him.

Malcolm looked from Gerard back to the shaven-headed man, then pulled out a chair, dropping into it and relaxing back.

"Well, we only spoke over the phone - Gerard, isn't it?" He said back to Gerard, who raised his bottle in reply.

"Do you care for a drink, Mr Willis?" the woman asked.

"No, you're alright doll, I'm fine. Erm … don't I know you? You seem very familiar." Malcolm replied, eyes lingering on her.

"Not personally, I assure you, sir." the woman said.

Malcolm was sure he knew her face.

"Then why do I feel like I do?" He asked.

The shaven-headed man leaned forward, and pushed a laminated DVD-sleeve over to Malcolm.

"Maybe this will enlighten you." He said.

Malcolm looked to the man, then dropped his eyes to the sleeve and turned it around. It was the cover of adult film 'Fist Club'. He suddenly felt ashamed. The girl in question was none other than Justine Emmanuelle Donnelly - adult movie superstar, and also of course, the wife of their enigmatic host - Marcus Donnelly.

"Forgive me - I can be a little slow on the uptake sometimes." He confessed, trying to shift the sudden memory out of his head of the *countless times he'd rubbed one out* watching her movies. Although he wasn't familiar this one, a porno parody of Fight Club.

Marcus smirked, sensing Malcolm's embarrassment, "Well ... at least that doesn't seem to hinder your professional work. I'm very pleased you were able to get that message to my friend here." Marcus replied, then stood up, "So without further ado, shall we, Mr Jones?"

Marcus Donnelly stood at over six feet and was well built, and with his shaven head, posed an intimidating sight. But Malcolm already knew what kind of man Marcus Donnelly was. The only son of the late, much feared Mob leader Frank Donnelly; Marcus in little over three years had gone from an insignificant small time hood, to big-time gangster whose brand of organised crime was fronted by a chain of prestigious night clubs.

Gerard Jones placed his beer on a small table, then got up and walked over to the door, "Well, what are we waiting for - if you'll follow me gentlemen? I have a vehicle parked outside." He said, then opened the door and left.

Soon they exited the club and walked through a rear car park, Malcolm walking alongside Marcus as Gerard, keeping good to his word, led the way. They reached his black van, and Gerard opened the back twin doors with a set of keys to reveal a large, canvas hold-all sitting inside.

"Wasn't parking the van here a little reckless?" Malcom remarked, "Anyone could have ripped you off.".

Marcus smirked, "Nobody is dumb enough to jack a vehicle on my property, I assure you Mr Willis. I've got CCTV, gorillas on the doors, and eyes everywhere. You'll soon learn that if you come and work with me."

"Quite the man, aren't you Mr Donnelly?" Malcolm retorted, and Marcus shot him a look, as if to say *'You fucking with me asshole??'*.

"Well, no matter what you've got hooked up out here, bein' seen out in the open like this ain't good for nobody." Gerard interrupted, "So let's get back inside and make with the countin'." - he then grabbed the hold-all out of the van, and closed the doors.

Marcus then suddenly grabbed the bag, which Gerard was reluctant to let go of.

"I'll take it from here, Mr Jones - you've done well enough sitting on this for me all this time."

Gerard stared at Marcus, then relinquished his hold, and Marcus walked away with it, leaving just Malcolm and Gerard to look at each other before separating.

"Hey - don't I get my share?" Gerard called.

Malcolm hurried to catch up with Marcus, who called back to Gerard as they returned to the club.

"I'll be in touch, Mr Jones." He said, then entered with Malcolm, as Gerard sighed, locking the back of his van, before walking around to the front and climbing in.

CHAPTER 5

The following morning, Cameron was sitting up in bed, with her cell phone to her ear, an early morning sun beaming in between the drapes to partially light her room. After a few rings the other end picked up.

"Davina? It's me - I can't be long, just got something to tell you." She said, purposely keeping her voice low in case of anyone overhearing.

In Davina's apartment, Davina paced the floor with the telephone cord dangling across the living room. She was dressed in a flimsy grey t-shirt and little else.

"What is it? Have you got some good news for me? Tell me you have, Cam'." She replied, her hand shaking as she clutched the receiver to her ear.

"Don't worry - I saw Gerard last night, and well, he's managed to give me some stuff - but I can't really say much over the phone." Cameron's voice answered.

"Really? Er, when you b-bringing it over?" She urged, grimacing as stomach cramps sent a spike of pain.

Cameron played with her lip-ring as thoughts raced through her head, and she recalled the previous night ... especially the feeling of Gerard on top of her and the fact he needed to trim his fingernails.

"Well, maybe later tonight - he wants me to go over again after work - I could get some more off him then too."

"So... I'll see you tonight, huh?" Davina breathy voice asked with desperation.

Cameron paused, and could feel tears welling up in her eyes, "Don't worry - just keep away from any of that fuckin' shit you got off your neighbour, and I'll... I'll bring you the good stuff."

Davina walked out into the hallway and stopped by a table where her telephone was situated. She steadied herself against the wall.

"Alright - I'll hold out until you come over - er, Cameron?"

"Yeah?"

"I love you - you know that?"

Cameron smiled. Hearing such from Davina was enough to cause a tear to escape and roll down her cheek, "I love you too, babe." She replied quietly, then lowered the phone.

Love can make a girl do crazy things, she mused as she ended the call.

*

Over an hour later, Cameron strode across the courtyard at the back of the hostel, where youths stood around either smoking or playing basketball. She approached Gerard from behind who was standing by the wire-mesh fencing, talking to a teenage Chinese girl the other side.

"OK, you meet me here the same time tomorrow, and I'll have something for you." He whispered, then sent her on her way.

He then turned to see Cameron, "Oh, hello treacle - what you up to? Not soaked up all that scag already have we? But I suppose I might have time for a blowjob, if you're quick." - he started to unfasten his belt.

Cameron shoved him, "For fucks sake, Gerard. No, I haven't touched it - er, keeping it for a rainy day, you could say." Cameron replied, disgusted by the way he referred to their arrangement, "So, who was that? Not peddling your wears in work time, are we?"

Gerard smirked, "What can I say - a chap's gotta make 'ends-meet."

Cameron turned away with a sigh, "I've got laundry to do - I'll speak to you later." She said, and went to walk off.

"Hey, wait up!" Gerard exclaimed, grabbing her arm, "You must 'ave come over 'ere for a reason - you know I don't like us being seen together."

Cameron looked around, but the kids were blissfully ignorant to them, "I just thought I'd see if things are still on for after." She replied unconvincingly.

"You bet they are. After last night?"

Cameron failed to hide her disappointment.

"I've got it all arranged - candles, scented oil, incense..."

Cameron pictured the scene, and almost felt attracted to it.

"Really?" She replied, creasing up her brow.

"Dream on, love - that stuff is for fuckin' pussies like Sting. You know how it's always going to be with me...I ain't ever bullshitted you about that, and I ain't going to start now."

Cameron looked disturbed, then turned and walked away.

"Hey - what did I say?" He called after her, then chuckled to himself.

* *

That afternoon, just after two o'clock, Malcolm arrived at the entrance gates to a mansion, and a security guard came out of a small cabin. He couldn't help but offer a look of admiration at Malcolm's chosen mode of transport - a sleek black Porsche 911 Turbo.

"Erm, can I help you sir?" He asked.

Malcolm's window was down, and Bonnie Tyler boomed from the in-car CD system. He lowered the volume a touch, then poked his head out.

"Malcolm Willis. Mr Donnelly will be expecting me, pal - just open the gates."

The guard looked insulted, and soon disappeared back inside his cabin. Malcolm hired up Total Eclipse of the Heart, and watched the guard on a phone, until eventually the gates opened, and he revved his engine before accelerating up the long driveway.

Marcus' mansion was a large white building in the middle of several acres of land, but considering Malcolm had grown up surrounded by wealth, it didn't seem as impressive as it would to the average person. He parked his Porsche in a drive way at the front of the house, next to a white Limo and a Jaguar XKR sports car.

On leaving his car, a young valet-parking attendant rushed over, "I'm sorry sir, but Mr Donnelly insists that all vehicles are looked after by myself." He said, holding out his hand.

Malcolm slowly lay his keys into the valet's hand, pausing, "I'm sure you're very experienced with cars my friend, but let me tell you now ... they are a particular passion of mine - so treat her like that friend you gave a reach-around to in college, and me and you will get along fabulously."

The valet stood looking shocked, and Malcolm walked away, smirking to himself as he approached the large front doors of the mansion, stone pillars standing either side.

Soon Malcolm was lead down a corridor inside the house, where vintage movie posters from the 50's and 60's adorned each wall, titles like 'The Blob' and 'Faster Pussy Cat, Kill, Kill' encased in glass.

"Mr Donnelly is a little indisposed at the moment sir," said a Hispanic maid going by the name 'Catalina'.

Malcolm came to a wide doorway that led into a grand living area, and a large TV screen was fixed to a wall playing cartoons with the sound down whilst subdued rock music played from an unseen music system.

"Mrs Donnelly will be keeping you company, if that's alright, sir." Catalina added, then walked away as Malcolm entered the room to see Justine Emmanuelle Donnelly slouched attractively on a white, soft-leather sofa, in nothing but a flimsy two-piece bikini.

"We meet again, Mr Willis." She said, sipping a

glass of sparkling champagne.

She was an instantly sexy sight, but in total contradiction to the usual Pornstar look; not a hint of silicone, and with her cropped black hair, minimal size and small breasts, she reminded him of an ex-girlfriend.

"Hello again, Mrs Donnelly - erm, you just been in the pool?" He asked, noticing on closer inspection how her milky-white skin was a little wet, and her hair glistened.

"How did you guess?" She replied with a grin, "Care to join me for a drink?" - she got up, and walked over to a bar, and grabbed a glass from behind that matched her own.

From where Malcolm took a seat on the sofa, he was able to ogle her perfect arse, presented in the G-string of her bikini bottoms. Gazing upwards he then noticed a tattoo running up her spine, a design of various musical notes.

"I'll have whatever you're having." He said appreciatively, and Justine, so very aware of the arousal she could infect a man with, smiled as she poured him some bubbly.

"Marcus should be down in a moment - he's with a friend of mine, Yuki Nada, have you heard of her?" She said, as she returned to the sofa, then handed him the glass before reclining again.

"No - is she someone famous?" Malcolm replied, trying not to stare.

"Well yes - she won best actress last year at the Hot D'or festival in Cannes."

"Oh ...I see."

Justine smirked, enjoying the moment "Does it embarrass you Mr Willis, knowing what I do for a living?"

"Embarrass - no, er, not at all - living and growing up in LA, you learn to accept the unusual."

"Is what I do for a living unusual to you?"

"Well, maybe 'unusual' was the wrong word."

"Have you ever seen one of my films?"

"Your movies? Er, no." Malcolm lied, then gulped down some champagne as if to quench his nerves rather than his thirst.

"Well, you don't know what you're missing. I could arrange for you to watch a shoot sometime. It's not as glamorous as people think, but seeing two girls going at each other covered in baby lotion, well, it will get you hard in less than a second."

Malcolm glanced around the room, which was beautifully decorated, but a bit too art-deco for his taste, with pastel grey walls and no drapes on the windows. Above a fireplace he also noticed a distinctive mural, depicting the signs of the zodiac painted in a circle.

"That's quite an offer, Mrs Donnelly. I'll give it some thought."

"Call me Justine, please." She replied, adjusting her position on the sofa, and sat up on her knees, leaning away to place her glass on a table, before then running her hand up the front of Malcolm's shirt.

"Care for a preview?" She asked.

Malcolm looked at her as her hand then dropped to between his legs and she ran her fingers over a gradually increasing bulge in his pants. Simply the smell of her sweat was almost too much.

"I... don't think so." He replied, and quickly got up, turning his back on her.

"Oh come on, Mr Willis" Justine added, "You wouldn't be treading on anyone's toes I can assure you - what do you think Marcus is doing with my friend Yuki - discussing fine wine and literature??" Justine added.

Just then, Marcus entered the room wearing a bathrobe, and Malcolm gulped at how close he had just come to accepting the woman's offer.

"Not annoying our guest, are you Justine?" Marcus announced.

A disappointed looking Justine slouched back down on the sofa, pulling a jib like some spoilt schoolgirl.

"Sorry I wasn't here to greet you, Malcolm." Marcus then continued as Malcolm looked at him, his arousal mercifully fading.

"Oh that's alright." He replied, taking another swig of champagne, "I assure you, your wife has been the perfect host."

Marcus came close to Malcolm, lowering his voice, "Well, I've just had the pleasure of savouring a far-Eastern delicacy."

"Pardon?"

"In English, that means I've been screwin' a Chinese girl."

Malcolm couldn't help but feel uncomfortable at how the two of them paraded their sexuality like a coat of arms.

"Well, are we gonna talk business, Mr Donnelly?" He retorted, eager to change the subject.

"Ah, a man after my own heart - of course, Malcolm - please, follow me..." Marcus answered, then looked to his wife, "If you want, I think Miss Nada is still relaxing in the Jacuzzi. Why don't you join her?"

Justine looked away - her ego had been too well bruised to settle for second prize.

CHAPTER 6

Marcus led Malcolm into an office elsewhere within the labyrinth layout of the vast house, and took a seat behind a large oak desk. He tidied some DVD cases into a drawer, then produced a soft blue folder.

"Alright. These are the deeds for the bar. Now what this means is that you are willing to invest an agreed sum of money into Tombstone, and therefore, we shall be joint owners - partners you might say."

Malcolm sat down in a chair in front of the desk, and crossed one leg over the other.

"When it comes to money, I don't kid around, Marcus." He announced, then retrieved a gold pen from inside his suit jacket, "So just show me the dotted line."

Marcus stared at Malcolm sternly.

"I've read up on you, Malcolm, I think you should know that, and I see where you're coming from. When is the earliest you can come up with the money?" He asked.

"I can sign a cheque right now, if you like."

"That won't be necessary. I have people for that sort of thing. I guess there's no reason to not welcome you aboard, then."

Marcus slid the file over to Malcolm, who opened it, and scanned the small print, "Will there be a manager, or is there one already?" He inquired.

"One of my friends is running the joint at the moment, but as of Monday, and when my accountant has verified the transaction, you will officially be calling the shots."

"I like the way that sounds Marcus. Where do I sign?"

"On the dotted line, just like you said."

Malcolm then leaned forward and scribbled his signature on the allocated line. Marcus grinned his approval.

A knock then came to the door. Marcus looked over as Malcolm finished signing.

"Who is it?"

"Marcus, there's one of your goons on the phone - you want me say you're busy?" came Justine's voice.

"Nah, its OK honey, I'll take it in here." Marcus called back, then lifted a telephone receiver built into the desk, and pressed a number.

"Donnelly here - what's up?" He said.

Malcolm watched and listened, seeing Marcus nod then look troubled, before hanging up.

"Problems?"

"You're gonna be part of the family now, Malcolm, and I'm sure you understand the responsibilities that comes with."

Malcolm nodded.

"Well, there seems to be a problem with the money Gerard was holding."

"What kind of problem?"

Marcus couldn't help but look frustrated, "Bruno, one of my best guys - I think you've met him already - big fella. Well, he has been counting it, and erm, he's discovered that every penny, every last note, looks to be fake - you know, counterfeit. All the cash has the same damn serial numbers n' shit."

Malcolm was shocked.

"So I'd appreciate it, as a mark of our new friendship, if you'd help me out on this matter Malcolm. Track down Mr Jones once again and get me some fuckin' answers."

"That son-of-a-bitch. I'll get right on to it." Malcolm agreed.

"If you like, I'll have Bruno and Dennis help you out - I know what kinda fly boy this guy can be sometimes. Fuckin' thinks he's Marlon fuckin' Brando he does."

*

Just after five p.m. that evening, Gerard exited the hostel with Cameron, and approached his van, which was parked on the road.

"Now I don't want to hear another word about things you have to do tonight." Gerard said to Cameron as he walked around to the driver's side, and unlocked the door.

"But Gerard, I'm not lying, I've got this thing on, with my sister - it's special like, because... she hasn't been home long." Cameron said as Gerard climbed in and reached over to unlock her side.

With reluctance she opened the door and jumped in, then Gerard suddenly grabbed her with his hand to her throat.

"Anyone would 'fink you don't want me to fuck you. But how else you going to score? A little rich girl like you, 'aving to go to some back-street dealer? Oh, what a family scandal that would make, and you bein' such the innocent an' everything." He snarled.

Cameron squirmed, but kept her cool, just thinking of Davina.

"OK, alright, I won't say anymore." She agreed as Gerard slowly removed his hand then started up the engine.

A short distance down the road, a large 4X4 Jeep started up, with two Black guys inside.

"This is it, they're on the move." the muscular one at the wheel announced, the same guy Malcolm had originally met in the underground car park.

"Who's the piece of ass? The boss never said anything about some cooze." his smaller friend added.

"Dunno - just a piece of white trash. All we're interested in, is tailing this dude then finding out where his crib be at. Then we report back. Simple."

"Let's do this then."

The jeep pulled out from a row of cars and drove off after the van - keeping a good distance so not to be spotted.

A little while later, the jeep arrived across the street from the apartment building where Gerard was staying, and it had begun to rain lightly, enough to form puddles on the sidewalks.

"Right Bruno, I'll go in, and report back via phone." the small Black guy by the name of Dennis explained, then opened the door and jumped out.

Bruno kept the engine running.

On the ninth floor of the somewhat upmarket apartment building a few minutes later, an elevator opened and Dennis came out, looking up and down the corridor, then heard footsteps. He quickly hurried towards a fire exit, and disappeared into a stairwell just as Gerard came around the corner with a newspaper under his arm and a four pack of beer held in one hand.

Dennis peered out through the gap in the door, and saw Gerard stop at an apartment.

"Gotcha." Dennis whispered.

Back at the Jeep, Bruno revealed his cell phone as it rang out - Dennis's grinning face came up as the contact picture. Bruno quickly answered it.

"What you got for me, cuz?" He said.

Dennis returned to the elevator and pressed the call button, "Our boy is in apartment 35A, on the ninth floor." He reported into his own phone.

"Excellent, man - now get your ass down here." Bruno's voice replied, and the elevator doors opened, allowing Dennis entry.

* *

As it turned 6:30 p.m. Malcolm's Porsche arrived next to the Jeep, and both vehicles lit up the rain-swept street as darkness fell.

"I'll take it from here, boys." Malcolm said with his window down.

Bruno looked in at him, "Are you sure, man? I've heard this one can be a pretty tough motherfucker."

"That streak of piss? No it's fine, tell Mr Donnelly I'll be in touch." Malcolm concluded, then drove away, and turned into the entrance of the building's underground car park, disappearing from view.

Minutes later, Malcolm left the elevator on the ninth floor, and walked down the corridor until he reached apartment 35A. He approached the door, and pressed his ear against it, until he heard music.

Inside, Gerard was slouched in an armchair wearing just a pair of underpants, a light layer of perspiration coating his body all over as he wiped a crimson smear from the knuckles of his right hand. On the floor lay a mattress, where a discarded set of handcuffs could be found along with a black silk blindfold.

In the hallway of the apartment meanwhile, the door clicked open, then brushed the thick pile carpet as Malcolm crept in. This was it, he thought as he returned his lock-picking kit to his jacket's inner pocket, then silently proceeded towards the living room, passing a door on the way that stood ajar. This was the reason he'd turned to a man such as Marcus Donnelly. Malcolm had craved the kind of underworld excitement that no Playboy lifestyle was ever likely to deliver.

Inside the bathroom, Cameron in just a bra and

thong stood before a mirror, holding a tissue over her mouth and nose, soaked through with her blood. In addition to this, a deep bite mark scarred the back of her leg just under her left buttock. Tears stung her eyes, and her body was aching from head to toe. It had been another rough encounter with Gerard, and the scars were beginning to show, both physically and emotionally. Suddenly, she flinched as an almighty crash was heard, and she turned around in alarm as Gerard's voice was heard.

"How the fuck did you get in here?" He shouted as Malcolm held him against the wall as a standard lamp toppled over.

"That's insignificant, pal - I want answers and I want 'em now!" Malcolm replied, enjoying the act of aggression a little too much.

Cameron approached the bathroom door from inside, and peered out, shocked on recognising her brother's voice. She lowered the tissue to reveal a bloody nose and a split lip.

"What are you talking about? Did Marcus send you?" Gerard gasped wide eyed.

"Have you tried to screw him, Gerard? Have you!? You really better not have, or this will get ugly real fast."

"I fuckin' swear I have no fuckin' clue what you are talkin' about. What's the problem? I fuckin' gave him his money!"

"Oh yes, you gave it to him alright." Malcolm said, then pulled Gerard away from the wall, and pushed him down into an armchair.

As Malcolm moved away, regaining his composure, he nearly tripped on the mattress, and looked down at it with a raised eyebrow.

"You been havin' a little party up here, buddy? What unfortunate bitch you been screwing then?"

"Oh, nobody you'd know. Just some whore I picked up." Gerard replied, catching his breath.

In the bathroom, Cameron felt nervous and also insulted, moving away from the door.

"Well never mind that now." Malcolm said, picking up the handcuffs and examining them, "I want a simple answer from you Gerard. So think before you reply. Did you know the money was counterfeit when you handed it over?"

"What?? Counterfeit?? That's impossible!"

Malcolm tossed the cuffs onto a sofa, then took a pair of leather gloves from his suit jacket, and began to put them on slowly.

"I swear on my mother's life, I had no idea! How can it be? Did the guys we robbed pull a fast one?"

Malcolm didn't reply, and as a result, his silence was more threatening.

"Listen - if I was tryin' to blag this, don't you think

I'd be gone by now? Why would I hang around for someone like you to show up and do me in?"

Malcolm sighed, "Would you be willing to tell Donnelly that, if I called him?" He asked, then took out his cell.

"Sure, mate - just dial the fuckin' number."

Cameron meanwhile slowly sneaked out of the bathroom, and slipped into the master bedroom without anyone seeing. Inside she hurried to the bed, where her tracksuit was slung, and she began to dress.

Malcolm passed Gerard the phone, and he sat up, "Hey, Marcus - it's Gerard. Now listen. Fuck. I know how this looks man, but I think we've been set up. Maybe a decoy was deployed, because someone somewhere knew the truck was gonna get hit, so we ended up with the Mickey Mouse shit instead of the real thing."

Malcolm watched him, and had to admit, Gerard was quite convincing. He almost felt sorry for the poor cockney.

"OK, I'll tell him that - and hey, thanks, Marcus - I owe you one." Gerard concluded, then passed the phone back to Malcolm, who switched it off and concealed it again.

"So he cut you some slack, huh? I think you better count yourself very lucky."

"I swear man, I hardly looked at the stuff - I just had it in a lock up, where nobody could get to it. The idea was to keep hold of it till the noise settled. So I just did as I was told."

Malcolm turned away, "Well, I'll let myself out." He said, and walked into the hallway where the front door stood open.

"Erm, yeah, but hey, Donnelly told me he'd call you in the morning to discuss business." Gerard added.

Malcolm didn't reply.

CHAPTER 7

Gerard put on a bathrobe and secured the rope belt before leaving the living room. Inside the master bedroom, Cameron flinched in reaction to a knock on the door, and she pulled on a white sleeveless vest, then reached for her tracksuit top.

"Can't a girl have some privacy?" She called out as she pushed one arm at a time into her sleeves, before eventually zipping up the front.

"What are you doing in there? Do you want me to fix you some coffee?" came Gerard's voice.

Cameron sat down on the bed, where crumpled sheets lay haphazardly, and reached down to her sneakers, mumbling under her breath as she slipped one foot in.

"Do I want a coffee..." She quietly mocked, starting to tie the laces.

Gerard walked away when he didn't get a reply, and glanced into the bathroom, where Cameron had left her blood-stained tissue on the washing basin, and the tap was running. He entered and turned it off, then looked at his reflection, noticing some stubble on his chin.

Back in the bedroom, a now fully-dressed Cameron carefully removed the ring suddenly irritating her lip, and went to place it on a cupboard next to the bed, but instead it slipped out of her hand, falling to the floor and rolling underneath. She cursed as she saw it disappear from sight, and sank onto her knees to search after it. She felt under the cupboard with one hand, then frowned as she came across what felt like a sheet of paper. Immediately she pulled it out, and to her surprise, discovered it to be some sort of map, with a location drawn rather artistically, of a cemetery. One particular grave was marked with a red 'X', and this couldn't help but intrigue her. Gerard was then heard knocking on the door again, and she quickly hid the map under the pillow as the door opened.

"Are you about ready? If you like, I can call you a cab." He said.

"Just give me a minute, yeah?" She replied, sitting back on the bed and grabbed a bottle of Budweiser off the top of the cupboard.

As she put it to her mouth, she winced as the cold rim touched her bruised, split lip. Gerard noticed and stared at her - *maybe this time things had got a bit rough*, he thought. He liked Cameron, in a very guarded way, and did want things to continue, and not just for the sex.

"Hey, I erm, I'm sorry honey, er, does that hurt?" He said, walking towards the end of the bed, "You know how I get when dropping acid and fuckin' at the same time."

Cameron turned her face away, then looked to the pillow, where she noticed a corner of the map peeking out. She was quick to pull the pillow towards her.

"Hey, don't be worryin' about that." She replied, "Didn't I say I liked it rough?" - she felt like she was reading an auto-cue.

Gerard smirked, "I'll make us a coffee, and then we're shooting off." He said, and turned around, then walked out, taking care to close the door behind him.

As Cameron held the bottle in her hand, she sighed at her situation, hardly believing she was right back in it once again. Yet she'd cocked up what had seemed like her only escape so spectacularly, that it now felt like she was trapped - but she'd endure it, if only to ease the suffering Davina was going through. Cameron couldn't bear to see her friend like that, and was prepared to do anything to help her, no matter the cost.

She took a lengthy swig from the bottle, then placed it back on the cupboard, where she then caught sight of a filing tray with a dozen or more blank sheets of note paper. She furrowed her brow as a rather devious idea occurred to her, and something she overheard when she was in the bathroom, repeated itself in her head...

"I want a simple answer from you Gerard. So think before you reply. Did you know the money was counterfeit when you handed it over?"

Without hesitation, she grabbed a sheet of paper and a pen, then pulled the map out from under the pillow. She got down from the bed, and turned around, using the firm surface of the mattress to sketch the map out onto the note paper, using her talent for drawing to include every little detail, especially the location of the grave marked with a red-cross.

Once finished, she turned the map over, eager to find out where the cemetery was actually located, and written in red ink, was 'Parkvale Cemetery & Crematorium - Knight's Bridge Avenue, East LA'

She wrote that on the back of her copied-out map then folded it up, concealing it inside her tracksuit pocket.

"Cameron? Coffee is ready, sweet 'art." Gerard then called, and Cameron quickly shoved the original map back under the cupboard, before standing up and hurrying to the door.

She entered the kitchen seconds later, with an innocent smile on her face, as Gerard handed her a mug, steam rising into the air above it.

"Gonna take me forever to clear all that junk in the

living room you know." He announced.

"Well, I'd love to stick around and help," Cameron said, "but my folks, they have been trying to impose this curfew on my ass, but so far I've managed to waver it - although I wouldn't like to push things."

"Curfew? How bloody old do they think you are? You're 23, an adult. If you can get into a fuckin' club, why on earth shouldn't you be able to stay out as late as you want?" Gerard reacted with disapproval.

"A little something about getting arrested for breaking & entering. My dad being a Judge an' all, something like that don't go down too well."

Gerard sympathised and took a sip of his coffee, as Cameron glanced around the kitchen.

"But maybe I have time for a biscuit." She added with a glint in her eyes.

Gerard smiled.

*

An hour later, a door opened into a room inside a hotel overlooking Venice Beach, and Malcolm crept inside, silently removing his shoes as he closed the door behind him. Suddenly, the lights of the main room came on, to reveal a disgruntled looking Jeanie standing by the light switch.

"Alright Malcolm, I want some answers." She said

sternly.

Malcolm looked like a child caught with his hand in the cookie jar, but finally gave in to his normally winning smile. Jeanie's look of suspicion and anger didn't shift. She was wearing a hotel bath robe.

"Well, OK babe, I suppose it's alright now for you to know what's been going on."

"We first came back here because of your sister, and I had no problem with that, but our home is in New York. Why if we're staying on, haven't I hardly seen you all week? You found someone else? Is that it, Malcolm? You slip your hands under some two-bit skirt when you went clubbing after Patricia's welcome home party?"

Malcolm sighed, and removed his suit jacket, "Not this again, Jeanie - I haven't been messing around behind your back, or anything like that. In fact, I've been trying to get some business to fall our way."

"Oh yeah?" Jeanie mused, intrigue slowly replacing her suspicions.

"With that in mind, how about you ordering us up two bottles of disgustingly expensive Champagne? 'Cause what I've got to tell you, is reason to celebrate."

Jeanie stern expression then gradually transformed into delight.

As the evening drew in, both Jeanie & Malcolm

lay in each other's arms on a leather sofa, totally intoxicated, and with only a little Champers left, kept ice cold in a frosted bucket.

"So, tell me my love..." Jeanie asked playfully, "Who is this man you're going into partnership with? Is he as handsome as you?"

Malcolm smiled wallowing in the moment, "Well, I can't comment on his looks in comparison to myself." He said with a snigger, "But he has clubs all over the United States, and he's filthy rich - so I think you and I are gonna feel right at home."

Jeanie grinned and emptied her glass with a final swig. She then placed the glass on a table and turned to look at her fiancé, just as he planted a loving kiss on her lips.

CHAPTER 8

That night, Edward Willis sat in his study at the family home, and was typing on a laptop. He was a silvery haired man in his early sixties, with a bushy moustache and prominent, thick eyebrows. Then the door creaked open, and Barbara crept in, placing a mug of Cocoa on the desk.

"It's getting late dear, shouldn't you be calling it a night?" She asked, wearing an embroidered dressing gown.

"This man who was on trial today, well, he was found guilty despite my better judgment." Edward related, still typing, "And I'd thought I'd just add something about it for my weekly article for the LA Times. Naming no names, of course."

"Did you think he was innocent? What was he charged with?"

"Murdering his wife and daughter. I know, it was an open and shut case, but I wished we could find out more, like what really lead up to the man doing such a thing. All the Jury seems to care about is reaching a quick verdict. It's not like it used to be, so much has changed since I first began."

Barbara noticed the text displayed on the screen, "The system is always changing - just think the way I do and move with the times. I'm sometimes representing very difficult clients. But it helps if you don't get too involved."

Edward sighed, pausing from his typing to take a sip of Cocoa, the glow of the laptop illuminating his face.

"Anyway, I think there's more important things than work at the moment, closer to home." Barbara continued.

"Such as?"

"Patricia's very concerned about Cameron. In her opinion she doesn't believe Cameron is being completely honest about staying out so late yesterday and today. Isn't she supposed to be on a curfew?"

"Curfew? I think you're forgetting dear, she isn't a child anymore." Edward replied.

"Yes, but part of the agreement when she was in court was that we'd keep an eye on her. She could be up to anything behind our backs."

Edward turned in his office chair.

"Do you want me to talk to her?" He asked.

"I dunno, will it do much good?"

"Maybe. I'll go now before bed." Edward said, placing his Cocoa on the desk, then got up.

Shortly afterwards, Edward met up with Patricia on the upstairs landing, who wore a white silk dressing gown to complement his own patterned smoking jacket.

"Oh Patricia. You're not in bed?" He inquired.

"No. I can't seem to sleep before 2am these days." She replied.

"I hope that's a joke." He said, then went to pass, "Er, Patricia - is Cameron still awake?"

"I don't know. When she came in, she went straight to bed. Why?"

"It's alright, I'll just go check."

Patricia watched him continue down the hallway, then descended the steps slowly on a single crutch.

Edward reached Cameron's bedroom door, and laid a knock on the wood. No answer came.

"Cameron, honey?" He called, then twisted the door knob.

The door clicked open, and he peered inside, where the room was presented to him in subdued lamp light, and the duvet was pealed back, the pillow flattened like the bed had recently been vacated.

"Cameron?" He whispered with concern.

In the on-suit bathroom, Cameron was seated on the toilet with the lid down, dressed in her underwear and nothing else as she held her cell phone to her ear.

"So, are you feeling any better?" She said into it.

At Davina's apartment at the same time, Davina lay in her bathtub, with soapy water up to her breasts, and one arm dangled over the side with a rubber tourniquet hanging slack from the elbow. She had a glazed look to her eyes, and her wet hair clung to her face.

"It's like being reborn." She breathed into a telephone receiver with the cord trailing across the floor and out through the open bathroom door, "So how about you? Are you naked? Tell me you're naked."

She heard Cameron laugh.

"No, I'm not naked. But you be careful - I don't want you fallin' asleep and drowning."

"Thank you, Cameron." Davina then said in all seriousness, "You've saved me ... yet again."

Then Cameron looked up as Edward said her name outside the door.

"Shit. I've gotta go, it's my Dad. Now, I'll see you tomorrow." She said, standing up to reveal a large plaster covering where Gerard had bitten her on the back of her leg.

"No problemo, sugar." Davina's breathy voice replied, then Cameron switched off the cell.

Soon she opened the door leading into her

bedroom, and had put on a dressing gown of similar style to her sister's. Her bruised and split lip was also strangely healed - although more than likely had just been disguised with make-up.

"Dad! I could have been naked!" She cursed on seeing Edward.

"I'm sorry - are you going to bed now? What were you doing, phoning one of your friends?" He answered, referring to the cell phone in her hand. Cameron quickly put the phone away in a drawer beside the door, then climbed onto her bed. She then winced as she felt the bite mark send a pulse of pain through her lower body.

"I was just checking my, er ... my messages." She replied, struggling to hide her discomfort.

Edward looked at her sternly.

"What is it, Dad?" She asked, crossing her legs and sitting on top of the covers.

"Are you OK? You looked in pain just now." He said.

"It's nothing - just a mishap at work - carrying too many boxes. It was my own fault."

"Well, your mother and I, we've been talking, and well, we're a little concerned, about these late nights."

"God, you do jump to conclusions, don't you? It's only been last night and tonight for Christ's sake!" Cameron snapped.

"Well, apart from that, you've also been very touchy and in a bad mood most the week. Don't you know if anything's bothering you, you can always come and talk to me?"

Cameron sighed, "Forget about it Dad - I'm just dandy. Probably doing this work at the hostel isn't exactly sending me home with a smile on my face - so it's only natural I should want to go for a drink, see a few friends once in a while, if only to keep my mind off the whole thing."

"And who are these friends?"

"Nobody you'd know."

"Not the same friends that left you at the pharmacy? They're not friends, Cameron."

"Agreed, they're not my friends - well, not anymore. But no, it wasn't them. Just some girls from the hostel."

Edward glanced around the bedroom, "So, you're OK, it's just this community work, yes?" He asked, eyes focusing on his daughter again.

"Yes Dad."

"Well, you've only got next week to go, and then it's over. But, just call us in future when you're going out - after all, I did promise I'd keep an eye on you."

Cameron smiled as her father walked to the door leading out into the hallway.

"I promise. Now can I go to sleep? I've still got to be up in the morning, at least for now."

Edward smiled back at her and nodded, leaving the room and closing the door behind him. Then once silence was restored, Cameron got up from the bed and went to the cupboard by her bathroom door. She knelt down and pulled open the bottom drawer, until it came out and she placed it on the floor, revealing an assortment of underwear, neatly packed in colour co-ordinated sections. Then she reached a hand into the compartment where the drawer had once been, and retrieved the copied map, folded up tightly. She opened it and looked at what she had drawn whilst sitting on her knees.

A big, excited grin slowly formed on her face.

*

Meanwhile, at Gerard's apartment, Gerard got up from his armchair to the sound of the doorbell, having been watching 'The Good, The Bad & The Ugly' - one of his favourite movies, on TV. He walked out into the hallway, and unfastened the locks, shouting at the buzzer all the time. When he opened it, he was met by three men dressed in suits, each of them Italian.

"Mr Leone!" He gasped in reference to the middle-aged gent standing with two younger, very well built men.

"Gerard!" the man replied with enthusiasm, "Not a bad time, is it?"

The man barged inside, and the two younger men pushed past Gerard as they entered. Gerard watched them proceed into his - now tidied -

living room, before closing the door and following. Inside, the middle-aged Italian had sat himself down in Gerard's chair, the two younger Italian's remaining either side like bodyguards.

"Erm, can I fix you guys a drink, at all?" Gerard offered, quick to mute the western on screen with a remote.

"No drinks, Gerard - just come and sit yourself down."

A little nervous, Gerard took a seat on the sofa near the armchair, and the middle-aged man took off a pair of spectacles, that he began to clean with a silk cloth, before putting them on again.

"OK, Gerard. I respect you, so I'll get straight to the point. It's been about a month since you informed me of that little incident involving Marcus Donnelly ... and a little bird tells me you've already made the switch. So now I'm thinking to myself; when is Salvatore going to be expecting a visit from you, to hand over your little gesture of friendship?"

"Well, I've been meaning to talk to Don Salvatore about that, Mr Leone." Gerard replied hastily, "You see, Marcus is no idiot, and quickly discovered that the money I gave him were a fugazi. So, he sent this geezer of his 'round here, but don't worry. You see, I managed to convince the guy I was as much clueless about the whole deal as Marcus was."

"Alright, alright - but how does that change things?" Mr Leone asked.

"Well, Don Salvatore will still get fixed up - you know how much this deal means to me. But I'll have to sit on it a while longer, just until I'm sure Marcus hasn't got anyone stalkin' me."

Mr Leone sat back with a loud sigh.

"Salvatore is a very patient man, Gerard, but even his famous kind streak has a limit if pushed too far. I'll inform him you'll deliver the money in seven days, am I making myself clear?"

"As crystal, Mr Leone, that should be perfect." Gerard agreed.

As he locked the door of his apartment following Mr Leone's exit, Gerard pondered the dangerous game he was playing. Yet he also knew that Marcus thought he was small time. That was soon going to change.

CHAPTER 9

(Saturday)

It was just turned two o'clock when a Mercedes Benz convertible arrived outside Marcus Donnelly's luxurious mansion. The valet parking attendant approached, then paused when he recognised Malcolm at the wheel, who was wearing a silk shirt patterned with illustrations of dragons and Chinese writing. Jeanie was seated beside him, sporting large designer sunglasses.

"Ah, Mr Willis. Sir wish me to park the car?" the valet asked nervously considering their previous encounter.

Malcolm opened his door and climbed out, then passed the keys into the valet's hand. The valet smiled, then caught sight of Malcolm's dark-haired fiancée as she walked around the front of the Merc' wearing a tight-fitting red blouse and Leather trousers. Her voluptuous shape obviously appealed to him.

"This is some place." Jeanie remarked as she took hold of Malcolm's hand, and the valet jumped into the Merc' and pulled away.

"Is it? I suppose - reminds me too much of my parents place." Malcolm replied, as they ascended the bright-white steps and reached the front door.

Malcolm went to ring the bell, but then the large white door opened to reveal the diminutive sight of Justine, wearing loose jogging bottoms and a cropped top.

"Malcolm! Please, come in." She said, in a spirited mood.

Malcolm entered, and Jeanie eyed up the girl with interest - she didn't really look the type to be associated with a multi-millionaire business tycoon, she thought. Perhaps she was one of the help - a fitness instructor, maybe?

"This must be your fiancée - aren't you going to introduce us?" Justine continued.

They stood together in the spacious foyer that had a marble floor with a staircase that ascended the wall to the immediate right, and doorways were situated to their far left.

"Of course, erm, Jeanie - meet Mrs Justine Donnelly - our host's lovely wife."

Jeanie was surprised and offered her hand. Justine took it, then lowered her head to lay a gentle kiss to the knuckles. Jeanie blushed.

"Nice to meet you, Jeanie - I'm sure we'll be good

friends."

Jeanie retrieved her hand slowly and smiled.

"For sure." She replied, then they were interrupted by a polite cough, and Malcolm turned to see Marcus Donnelly exit a doorway that Malcolm recalled led into a corridor on-route to the living room.

Jeanie took her eyes from the fascinating Justine in time for Marcus' arrival, and was pleasantly surprised. He was handsome, in a way, but she didn't care for his shaven head - yet there was an unmistakable quality to him that she couldn't put her finger on.

"Malcolm - so glad you could make it." Marcus said, "Please, follow me."

Soon they entered the living room that Malcolm had so disliked on first seeing, but was surprised to find vases of fresh flowers displayed, and a print of an oil painting hanging on one wall. It was almost like a different room. Obviously, it had had a woman's touch in the last twenty four hours.

"Drinks are the order of the day, I think." Marcus said, "Jeanie - Wine, or something else?"

Malcolm sat down where he had sat before, and Jeanie sat down with him, crossing one leg over the other.

"Erm - have you got any beer?" She asked.

Malcolm frowned, knowing Jeanie only ever drank at night.

"Of course - Justine, grab our guest a bottle out of the refrigerator, will you?"

Justine, who had lingered in the doorway, hurried away obediently, and Malcolm couldn't help but watch appreciatively as she left.

Malcolm was soon handed a Martini with a little plastic umbrella, and Jeanie swigged down her beer, like she had been craving it. He glanced from his drink to hers with confusion.

Marcus then sat down in an armchair, and lit a Cuban cigar on a gold Zippo, "Well, tonight's our busiest night, for the club. Are you interested in tagging along when I go over there?" He asked Malcolm.

"Sure. Jeanie and I can't wait to take a look at the place."

"Mr Donnelly - Malcolm tells me you have a few clubs all over the states. Do you try and visit them all, from time to time?" Jeanie interrupted.

Marcus smiled at her, "I do like to keep an eye on my various businesses, and all the financial figures come back to me at the end of the month, so I can check what club is doing well, and what club might need some fresh ideas thrown at it. Tombstone is one such club, that although it's only been open to the public little over a month, the Western theme has really taken off, and with the added backing of Malcolm here, it can only go from strength to strength."

Jeanie was warming to Marcus, and Malcolm knew it, as he quickly jumped into the conversation.

"Something like that, a Western theme bar, has been aching to be done for decades 'round here. I don't know about you, Marcus, but I still love those movies; The Searchers, The Wild Bunch, Pale fuckin' Rider. Classics."

Marcus smirked, but welcomed Malcolm's enthusiasm, "Well, I see you know your cinema. I have a private screening room, here - you and I should check out the 35mm restoration I've managed to obtain of 'Once Upon a Time in the West' - it's quite an experience."

After a while of casual conversation that soon graduated into jokes and laughter with every drop of alcohol consumed, Jeanie came out into the corridor, and walked unsteadily. She paused by a door and tried it, but it was locked. She moved on, until she came to an open door, and went to enter, then froze when she found Justine sitting on the toilet urinating, her jogging bottoms around her ankles.

"Oh, I'm sorry." Jeanie said, then stepped back out, turning away.

"Hey, it's alright - I'm finished now anyway." Justine said, pulling her joggers up then flushing.

Justine reached Jeanie from behind, and could smell the alcohol that lingered in the air. She herself had never been a big drinker.

"It seems you two are getting very acquainted with my husband. What do you think? He's quite the stud, isn't he?" She said.

Jeanie turned to face her, and was squashed against the door frame as Justine pressed herself closer.

"Well I er, I suppose... he's very nice. Those gold teeth caught my eye."

Justine smiled, her eyes exploring Jeanie's face, "I don't mind, you know. We regard it as a normal part of our marriage."

"Regard what?" Jeanie said, confused, the scent of her perfume intoxicating.

"Marcus sees it as a way of accepting what I do. If you want to have some fun with him, I'm sure it can be arranged."

"Wait a minute. Are you suggesting what I think you are?"

"What's the problem? You're seriously telling me Malcolm's the only one for you?" Justine replied, then Jeanie felt the girl's hand brush her thigh.

"Of course he is - we're engaged to be married!"

"That shouldn't stop you. You're shy, is that it?"

Jeanie then felt Justine's hand unbuckle the belt of her leather trousers.

"Hey! What do you think you're doing?" She gasped.

"Oh come on, I noticed the way you were looking at

me – are you not wondering what I taste like?"

Suddenly, Jeanie pulled away and slammed the bathroom door in the girl's face, leaving Justine alone in the corridor. She smirked in response, then walked back towards the living room.

*

At that time at a local shopping mall, Davina walked with Cameron.

"I'm not sure about this Cameron; I don't want you getting into trouble on my part." Davina remarked.

Because it was a Saturday, the place was full of people, and kids ran around, playing and being generally rather irritating. But Cameron was in a good mood, and even Davina's poor attitude couldn't ruin things.

"Hey, it'll be fine, and anyway, it's only short time for me on Saturday, so you won't get me in any trouble, I promise." Cameron replied, taking hold of her friend's hand, and walked her into a large beauty salon.

Cameron had dressed Davina in her cleanest top and pants (which wasn't easy), which wouldn't have done much if Cameron hadn't insisted on Davina washing her hair and wearing shades to disguise those bloodshot eyes. She herself had avoided the expensive gear that filled her wardrobes at home, so Davina wouldn't look out of place. Cameron had big ideas for the both of them.

They were in the salon for over an hour, and Cameron lay on a bench having her nails done by a young Black girl whilst Davina was treated to a full make over. By the time they left, Cameron looked stunning with her bright white hair braided, and Davina looked like a totally different person; her previously long brown hair cut and styled into a fetching bob, and was wearing subtle make up, making her feel alive for the first time in months.

The next port of call was a big name department store, where Cameron brought clothes for the both of them, and soon they were walking back through the mall, and heads turned as passers-by looked there way and guys whistled their approval. Cameron wore flared patterned trousers that were split from the ankle to the knee, as well as a white blouse with a waist coat that seemed to perfectly match her trousers. Davina was dressed in an elegant black trouser suit with a white satin shirt underneath. It suited her immensely.

"So... feelin' good?" Cameron asked.

"I guess - this feels good, being with you, but I dunno, wearing this stuff, it's like..."

"Like you're a new person?"

"No, like I'm no longer dying."

"Hey!" Cameron retorted, coming to a standstill near a Starbucks, "Don't be talking like that. You've gotta be more positive."

Davina glanced around, then removed her glasses. Her eyes had been done up, and her face was given colour with plenty of blusher, but her pale hands gave everything away, especially when they trembled noticeably.

She paused before speaking, as if afraid to do so, "Positivity is for disillusioned suckers who can't accept their fate. The clinic has said I may only have months, perhaps less - it's not clear really."

Cameron turned away, refusing to accept what she was hearing even though Davina had drummed it into her many times in recent weeks.

"Just stop it." She gasped, Davina's words too painful to tolerate, "Can't we just forget all that for one day and enjoy ourselves - please?"

After a moment, a guilty-looking Davina took Cameron by the hand again, then led her inside the coffee establishment.

"I'm sorry. You're right. Let's get a coffee and the creamiest of cream cakes - I'd shout you, but I didn't bring my Amex." She said, and Cameron grinned, squeezing her hand in her own as they approached the counter.

"So, why all this, why today?" Davina asked once they were seated at a table at the back, where they were allowed a little privacy.

Cameron stirred a spoon in her mocha latte with sprinkles. Two large cream cakes sat invitingly on a plate between them.

"I don't need to an excuse to treat you, do I?" She replied, placing the spoon on the plate before raising the glass and taking a sip.

"I shouldn't really complain - I'm lucky you're talkin' to me at all after how much I've hurt you."

Cameron licked the froth from her lips, "Well, that's all in the past. I'm really tired of being angry, with you or Patricia. I just want to be here in the now - here for you, and try and help you when I can. That's why … I've got something really important to tell you."

Davina frowned, running a finger around the rim of her iced Frappuccino, sensing something big was about to be announced.

"What is it? Damn, this whole outing has just stank of a secret agenda." She replied with intrigue.

Cameron took a courage building drink of her latte, then looked around, but everyone else seemed lost in their own little worlds.

"OK, it's like this - from what I can tell, Gerard has ripped off some guy, some big time gangster called Marcus Donnelly. You see, he's stolen some large amount of cash, and palmed Donnelly off with a load of knock off bills."

"Are you serious? Do you realise who Marcus Donnelly is?" Davina whispered back.

"I've got my theories. I overheard Gerard feeding

some bullshit story to my brother, who Donnelly musta sent 'round - I mean, if Mom and Dad had any idea the type of thugs Malcolm's associating with these days, they'd go crazy."

"So how do you know its bullshit?"

"Because, and get this ... I came across a little map - a literal treasure map - in Gerard's bedroom, and I took it on myself to do a little copy. It must be where he's stashed the real money, and he's probably just waiting for a safe time to go get it."

"How do you know he hasn't done so already?" Davina asked.

"Because Gerard's not stupid, that's why - he'll stay quiet for a while, to make Donnelly think he's the real deal, that he didn't know the money was fake. Then, when he's not being watched anymore - say, probably a week or so's time, he'll make his move - but by then it'll be too late."

Davina grinned wickedly, "Because we'll have already snatched the rug out from under his feet." She concluded, and Cameron nodded, taking another sip of her latte.

"That's brilliant, do you know that?" Davina continued, reaching out to pick up her cake.

Cameron nodded, "I'm through with Gerard Jones screwing me - it's high time I screwed him back." - she then watched Davina bite into the cake, getting cream all over her mouth.

CHAPTER 10

Towards the end of the afternoon, Patricia, wearing joggers and a loose-fitting top stood in her particularly girlie-looking bedroom before a king size bed, a cell phone to her ear.

"Come on, answer God-dammit!" She cursed, then the other end picked up.

"Yeah, what's up?" came Malcolm's voice.

"Malcolm - about bleedin' time - where have you been? I've been trying to call you all week, but your phone has either been switched off or the manager at the hotel says you can't be disturbed."

"Hey, sis, relax - I've just had a lot on - why? What's the problem?"

Patricia calmed herself, "OK - can we talk? You're not too busy to speak to me, are you?"

"Listen, I'm with Jeanie right now, and we're with an associate of mine - maybe we should talk later - I'll call you tonight."

Patricia sighed, taking a seat on the edge of her

bed. A copy of the local tabloid was laid out beside her showing an article with a photo of her, taken as she left the courthouse. The headline read: 'local socialite and former private detective Patricia Willis acquitted on murder charges'.

"No Malcolm, this is important - I want to talk about my future. I mean, mom & dad have been great an' all, but I've been considering going back to Chicago, or New York maybe, and see if I can get into the detective agency-thing again."

"Are you sure? It wasn't exactly fun times, if you recall."

"I know, but well ... it was me, wasn't it? It was what I was good at, and anyway, there's not much keeping me here."

"Well, I'll talk to you some more tonight, around eight or nine, OK?"

"Alright Malcolm - but don't forget." Patricia agreed.

"Just don't worry about it - everything's going to be fine."

Patricia lowered the phone, then switched it off just as she heard the sound of a car. She got up slowly and hobbled over to the window, where between the curtains she could see outside to the driveway, and a taxi cab had arrived at the front of the gates. She observed silently, seeing Cameron step out, then leaned closer to the glass to see who was in the cab, then as Cameron stepped back, she recognised Davina reach out, pull Cameron back by grabbing her arm, and kiss her on the lips.

Patricia's mouth dropped open, as a memory flashed in her head. She was slowly kissing Davina as they floated together in the mansion's heated swimming pool, but rather than the gentle kiss she had just witnessed, this was passion and pure physical lust that would forever be engraved on her conscience.

"Lyin' little bitch." She remarked, then stepped away and grabbed a steel crutch from beside the bed, before making her way to the door.

Seconds later, she reached the top of the staircase, and witnessed the front door open, and Edward was there to greet Cameron.

"I thought you finished early on a Sat…" He announced, then saw her braided hairstyle, "Dear God - what have you done to your hair?"

"What, you don't like it? Well sorry Dad, I'm no longer your little girl!" Cameron snapped back, then walked away and went to climb the staircase, until she saw Patricia giving her daggers at the top.

"Oh, hi Patricia - like the new look? If you don't I couldn't give a stuff!" She remarked, then hurried up, pushing past her sister, who nearly lost her balance until she grabbed hold of the banister.

"Where you been this time, Cameron?" She asked.

"Butt out, Patricia, I'm warning you!" Cameron

replied, walking down the hallway to her bedroom.

"Why should I? Scared I'll discover your deep dark secret?"

Cameron froze. Then she slowly glanced back to her sister.

"What's that supposed to mean?"

Patricia hobbled towards her.

"Let's go into your room." She said.

Confused and a little bit scared, Cameron complied, turning to her door and walking into her room. Once inside, Patricia pushed the door shut, before staring at her sternly.

"What gives, Cameron? You lied to me." She said accusingly.

"What? What are you blabbering about? I didn't lie to you!"

"Oh yes you did, you told me Davina was in prison ... and I've just now seen you with her when you got out of that cab."

Cameron gave a sigh of relief, paranoia over her current plans almost getting the better of her, then walked away, dropping some designer labelled shopping bags on the bed.

"OK, I suppose I did - but when the subject came up, I couldn't handle getting into another argument with you over her - so it was easier for me to say she wasn't around." She explained.

Patricia approached, "Did you think I'd just go running back to her? Is that it?"

Cameron paused, staring at her sister, "I dunno - maybe, but despite what you did, despite all the bullshit, you're both still important to me. So I felt it would be better if I kept the two of you apart."

Patricia couldn't help but sympathise with Cameron, and it went some way to ease the guilt that had eaten away at her for too long.

"Hey, I'm sorry. Truly I am." She said.

Cameron forced a smile, "What's there to be sorry about?"

Patricia grinned back, then Cameron walked over to her, and they embraced like the loving sisters they once used to be, and could possibly be again.

Patricia stepped back, "I like it … your hair that is." She said, then frowned when she noticed a swelling to Cameron's bottom lip, "What's this?" She added, stroking a finger over Cameron's mouth, making her step back in response.

"Oh that, huh, you'll never guess - there was this girl at the hostel who thought she could take a pop at me - after that, the ring hurt me so I took it out. My lip really ain't used to being without it."

Patricia looked into her little sister's eyes, as if looking for the truth.

"Are you sure everything's alright?"

Cameron nodded, "I'm having a ball, Patricia, honest." She replied unconvincingly.

*

That evening, a stretched Limo arrived outside the western theme bar of Tombstone, just outside of LA's downtown area. The men guarding the entrance were dressed elegantly in old Western clothing, and came to open the door of the Limo. Jeanie climbed out to hear loud music and voices coming from inside as her eyes reflected the neon lights. She was followed by Malcolm, who took her by the hand, stepping aside as Marcus climbed out, wearing a black leather tuxedo and a large Stetson hat, and Justine followed, wearing tight black denim and a bow tie.

"Well? What do you think?" Marcus asked Malcolm, raising his voice over the noise.

"What do I think? It's like Rio Bravo."

Marcus laughed, then led the way. They entered Tombstone through traditional swinging saloon doors, and feast their eyes upon an expansive interior; a large stage directly ahead where dancing girls dressed exactly like the girls of the era, complete with garters and frilly dresses, could be seen doing the can-can.

"Oh my..." Jeanie gasped, overwhelmed.

"You people want a drink? We've got everything, but please, let me treat you both to a few shots of the house bourbon." Marcus announced, as they approached a long bar.

Then as they reached it, Malcolm saw the waiter behind slide a glass across the surface, and it was expertly caught by an old, bearded cowboy at the far end, who downed it in one go. Malcolm couldn't help but smirk.

A little while later, Jeanie was more than a little intoxicated, a crowd having gathered to watch her down a row of shots. She had gone through eight, and there were only two left. Malcolm was watching her with a fair amount of concern, but Marcus was having a whale of a time, a bottle of Rum in his hand and his free arm around Justine. The crowd cheered as Jeanie went for the next shot, and despite her mouth and chin being soaked with spilt liquor, she gulped it down eagerly.

Malcolm sighed, then leaned close to Marcus, "I've gotta go and make a phone call." He said, then walked away, as the crowd moved in to see if Jeanie could make it through all ten shots.

Justine then left her husband's side, and Marcus took his eyes from Jeanie long enough to see his wife follow in Malcolm's footsteps.

Malcolm entered a corridor that drowned out the noise of the club, and retrieved his cell, switching it on then scanned the screen as it lit up.

Back at the Willis mansion, Patricia limped into her bedroom to the sound of her phone, and fell onto the bed, grabbing and answering it as she landed.

"Malcolm?"

"Hey Patricia. See, I said I'd call you back. I'm a man of my word."

"Hmm, yeah - I knew I could rely on you - well, you had time to think about what I said?" Patricia asked.

"Not really, but I kind of already know how I feel."

"... and that is?"

A door a few feet behind where Malcolm stood, creaked open, partially flooding music in, and Malcolm looked back as it closed again. Then as he went to reply into the phone, it opened a little way, and Justine peered in, eavesdropping.

"I can't see me going back to New York anytime soon. In fact, a real big business deal has fallen into my lap, and I'll probably be staying on for a while, if not for good."

"What? You can't be serious, you mean like, buy a house, you and Jeanie settle here? What kind of business would make you want to do that? I thought you hated L.A." Patricia replied, exasperated, as she sat up.

"I do hate L.A." Malcolm replied, as then a young couple in Western dress passed him by, and Justine moved from the door as they re-entered the bar, "But I've decided to invest some money in a bar I know of. It's hard to go into details over the phone, but this could be the making of me in this town, sis."

Patricia ran her free hand back through her hair, hardly able to believe what she was hearing.

"Well that's it then, I'll just have to go by myself."

"Don't do that, Patricia - you should come down here. The place would really blow your skirt up."

"Oh yeah, some impact on re-entering society I'll make, walking on crutches."

"If you feel like that, why are you even contemplating going back?"

Behind Malcolm, Justine entered the corridor, and unbuttoned the top of her denim jacket, exposing her cleavage as she approached.

"I don't know - I just want things to be like they were. When I was a Detective, I was somebody, I was alive - staying here just makes me feel like a nobody, just the spoilt little rich girl everyone used to mock through high school."

Justine suddenly wrapped her arms around Malcolm from behind, and he flinched as she grabbed his crotch. He looked over his shoulder to see her grin wickedly.

"Erm, Patricia? We'll continue this conversation tomorrow - but don't do anything rash - sleep on it."

"Alright Malcolm, I suppose I can do that.

Goodnight then." Patricia replied, then her phone cut off, and she moved it from her ear, staring at it in confusion.

Malcolm turned to Justine and saw the unmistakable look of lust in her eyes.

"Justine! What are you doing?" He asked.

"Don't ask questions." Justine replied, gripping the swell of his ass in both hands, and the combination of her perfume and obvious physical beauty were enough to make him meet her lips with his own.

Within seconds he thrust her against the wall, making her grunt, and began to kiss her, any thought of consequence absent from his mind. Gasping for breath, Justine momentarily moved her mouth from his to whisper in his ear.

"Not here. I know a place. This way." She breathed, then took Malcolm's hand and the two of them hurried down the corridor.

CHAPTER 11

Cameron entered the large garage built onto the rear of the Willis mansion. She was wearing a hooded overcoat as she stood at the top of a flight of stairs, and admired the collection of glamorous vehicles on view below. They ranged from luxurious Aston Martin and Mercedes, to top of the range sports cars from Ferrari and Lamborghini, most of which belonged to Malcolm.

Closing the door that led back into the house, she hurried down the steps and walked in front of the cars. A long Perspex window was built into the wall behind, and showed off the shimmering view underwater of the mansion's in-door swimming pool, its glow dancing on each car's polished bodywork. Cameron stopped in her tracks to delve a hand into her satchel, then pulled out a set of car keys, and pointed the remote, pressing a button, until a set of headlights lit up and the engine of a black Aston Martin Vanquish roared into life.

"Let's roll." She enthused, hurrying over to the

driver's side, opening the door and jumped in.

*

Back at Tombstone, Malcolm gradually opened his eyes to find himself lying haphazardly on an opened out sofa-bed next to Justine, and they were both naked. He pondered the moments before they passed out and he smiled to himself, before sitting up. Glancing to the sleeping beauty as she lay on her front, he again admired the tattoo running down her spine; musical notes styled like calligraphy. It complimented the illustration of an angel that adorned his own chest.

Getting up, he grabbed the red-silk sheet from the floor, and wrapped it around himself as he gathered his bearings. Luckily he was still wearing his Rolex, and was surprised to discover it had just turned 2:30 in the early hours of Sunday morning. Feeling his heart race as the reality of the situation dawned on him, Malcolm hurried over to a chair, where his clothes had been slung, and quickly grabbed his shirt, putting it on as he looked back to the bed. Lying in a pile beside it were Justine's clothes, topped off with her discarded bow tie.

"Sweet dreams hun." He whispered to her, then fastened the buttons on his cuffs before reaching for his trousers.

Down in the bar, Jeanie had crashed out in a chair

amongst a dozen more men and women who had all seen far too much alcohol. Behind the bar, Marcus was helping clear up, wiping some glasses with a towel as his staff busied themselves tidying the tables and sweeping discarded cans and crisp packets off the dance stage.

After a while, Malcolm walked in, the collar of his shirt uneven and his suit jacket draped over one arm.

"Hey, we missed you down here, buddy - where you been?" Marcus announced.

Malcolm noticed Jeanie immediately, but passed her by to take a seat next to the bar, where Marcus' Stetson was occupying one of the pumps. He could barely look his new business partner in the eye, and began to feel incredibly nervous - how could he possibly explain this one?

"It's alright, Malcolm, I saw Justine follow after you."

Malcolm raised his head to meet Marcus' stare, eyes wide.

"Come again?" He retorted.

Marcus smirked, "I hope you enjoyed her, Malcolm, because... there's never a repeat performance."

Malcolm looked surprised, then turned around, "You got any of that bourbon left?" He inquired.

"Sure." Marcus replied, revealing an almost empty bottle, and poured the remainder into a clean glass, "Knock yourself out."

Malcolm took the glass, then looked back to Jeanie. "She been like that long?" He asked.

"A couple of hours. Quite the party animal, and she sure likes her liquor." Marcus commented.

Malcolm nodded, not exactly in approval, but then again, he could hardly get angry at her, after what he had done.

* *

Cameron's 'borrowed' Aston Martin Vanquish arrived outside the gates of 'Parkvale Cemetery & Crematorium' on Knight's Bridge Avenue, East LA. The sleek motor stood out like a saw thumb where old beaten-up vehicles occupied the street otherwise. Cameron was at the wheel as a sleepy Davina examined the copied map, holding it with her hands in black fingerless gloves. Her hair was messy and the old woollen jumper she had on looked like it should've been thrown out years ago.

"I think this is it - there ain't no other." She remarked.

"Alright - let's get searching." Cameron added, then leaving the engine running but switching off the headlights, she opened her door and climbed out.

Within minutes, Cameron was scaling the wrought iron gates, then flipped her body over the top, tossing her satchel to the ground, before climbing down the other side.

"Now you." She said to Davina, who looked up nervously.

"I dunno - I'm not feeling so good." She said, and rubbed her hands against herself with her arms folded.

"What, are you cold?"

Davina stared at her, and her lips quivered. Cameron guessed she wasn't bluffing.

"Well, come on, if you get moving, you'll feel better for it."

Davina took a deep breath, then began to climb the gates, slowly with overly cautious footing.

Soon they marched through the Cemetery, passing gravestones and tombs, as Cameron read the map. An owl hooted in one tree and the two women felt like they'd just stepped onto the set of a horror movie.

"I think it's near here, somewhere."

"Are you sure? I think I'm gonna puke." Davina remarked.

Cameron stopped in her tracks. She sighed and turned to her friend. Then she reached into the top pocket of her overcoat.

"Well, I've come prepared, here have these –" She said, then revealed a small packet of pills.

"Hey, where did you get those?" Davina remarked,

looking ghostly pale in the moonlight.

"I swiped them from your bathroom. They're just Paracetamol - I couldn't find those pills you said the clinic gave you."

Davina looked apprehensive, "Oh I er … I must have thrown them out." and she snatched the packet out of Cameron's hand, popping two pills as they proceeded.

Eventually they reached a grave, and Cameron knelt down.

"What you doing? Giving the last rights?" Davina asked.

"There ain't no name, or any kind of engraving on here."

"So what?"

"It's unmarked." She continued.

"Fascinating - let's just do this." Davina added.

Cameron got back up, then looked around.

"Fuck! How could I be so stupid?" She cursed.

"What do you mean?" Davina asked.

"Hello? Shovels! How we gonna fuckin' dig up this thing?"

"Oh shit, yeah - erm, there must be some shovels around here somewhere."

Cameron walked away from the grave, stuffing the map into her pocket, then spotted a hut in the distance between two old, overhanging oak trees.

"Let's take a look in there shall we?" She said, picking her satchel back up, then walked away.

Davina sighed, still not feeling 100%, then followed. Cameron reached the old hut, and tried the door, but of course, it was locked. She then opened her satchel, and pulled out a small crowbar.

"Where'd you get that?" Davina asked, alarmed.

"Borrowed it from my Dad's toolbox, back at the house. Come on; give me a hand with this."

Cameron then pushed the narrow end of the crowbar between the door and it's frame work, then with Davina taking hold, they both pushed against it, until the wood split apart, and the door swung open with the high-pitched squeal of rusted hinges. Cameron gasped, then waved her hand in front of her face to clear the cloud of dust that was created.

Once the dust had settled, they both peered inside, to discover to their considerable joy, two large shovels propped up against a chair in the corner of the hut interior.

Before long, the two of them, with most of the work done by Cameron, managed to dig fairly deep into the grave, until eventually they hit a hard surface.

"We're here." Cameron announced.

Davina struggled to climb out of the grave, then sat

on the grass, panting loudly.

"I'm going to pass out." She gasped.

"Just hand me that crowbar, will you?" Cameron's voice called.

Davina caught her breath and looked around herself, "Where'd you put it?" She asked.

"It should be right there." Cameron shouted back.

Davina got up and looked around, then suddenly, the sound of a gun being cocked alerted her, and she looked back to see an old, overweight Security guard shine a light in her face whilst pointing a revolver.

"Hold it right there, lady!" He exclaimed.

Davina turned around to face him and raised both hands. Inside the grave, Cameron sat up on her knees, then looked up to see the glow of the torch.

"Jesus Christ." She whispered with disbelief.

"What are you doing here, Miss?" the guard asked, "You don't look like the grave robbing sort."

Davina just stared at him sternly.

"Answer me, or we'll have a situation." the guard added when Davina didn't reply.

Then she smiled, and looked at the revolver, held by a none too steady hand.

"You been in this job long, pops?" She asked.

"20 years this fall, Missy, now stay where you are, I'm warning you!"

"You ever killed anyone?"

"What kind of question is that?"

"I bet even if I made a break for it, you wouldn't have the guts to shoot."

"You wanna try me? Just shut your mouth, you're under arrest!"

"I don't think so." Davina then replied, and lurched forward, snatching the torch out of the guard's hand, then pushed the gun away, which went off, the shot echoing in the cool night air. The guard flinched in reaction, then Davina swiped the torch hard against his temple, and he collapsed to the ground unconscious.

Davina looked down at the guard, taking a moment to catch her breath as the torch light flickered, then turned back to the grave as Cameron called out.

"Davina? Davina! You alright? Christ girl, fuckin' answer me!"

As Cameron looked up, Davina then peered in with a wicked smile.

"They ain't taking me yet honey!" She announced, tossing the crow bar down to her, and Cameron caught it perfectly.

"What was going on up there?" She asked.

"Relax babe, I sorted it - now just pop that son-of-a-bitch open and let's get out of here - this place is starting to give me the creeps."

Cameron straddled what to her surprise, was actually a full-size coffin, and began to prize it open using the crow bar. She just hoped it was what she was expecting and not some long dead granny. After considerable effort, the lid finally came off and she slid it aside to reveal... a bulging hold-all, not unlike the one Gerard handed over to Marcus in the first instance.

"Jackpot!" She exclaimed, and Davina peered in, the torch lighting up the hold-all just as it was zipped open, revealing a mass of crisp $100 bills.

"Oh, now that's beautiful." Davina added.

CHAPTER 12

(Thursday)

5 days later

The bandage around Patricia's left foot was slowly unwrapped as she sat up against the pillows of her bed, looking at her Physiotherapist with anticipation.

"So, what's the verdict, Julia?" She asked.

A pretty Spanish woman in her mid-thirties rest Patricia's foot on her lap and smiled.

"It seems you have made a great recovery, Ms Willis."

Patricia grinned, "See, I told you I wouldn't be hobblin' around on those damn metal sticks for too long."

"I would be careful though, you did fracture your ankle bone quite badly when you were in prison, so I wouldn't recommend exerting yourself too much. Avoid uneven terrain or anything remotely cross country." Julia the Physiotherapist replied, then got up, and Patricia sat forward, swinging herself around and placing both feet on the carpet.

"Thank you, Julia ... you've been so wonderful during all of this."

Julia smiled then walked away, leaving Patricia alone in the room to contemplate her future, something she had become quite accustomed to doing in the past couple of weeks.

In the bedroom next door, Cameron had a suitcase on her bed, and was packing some clothing into it, placing sweaters, skirts and underwear neatly next to a bag of cosmetics and an Apple I-Pod. She was already dressed in Dungarees and a Baseball cap, her face locked in concentration as she contemplated the time ahead.

Then her phone rang to the tune of Hawaii 5-O, and she quickly rushed to the chest of drawers next to the bathroom door, and answered it.

"Hey..."

"Hey yourself... erm, so, you all set for tomorrow night?" came Davina's somewhat throaty-sounding voice.

"Yeah, sure I am, and you?" Cameron replied in a whisper.

"Well, kinda. I'm not really sure what to pack..."

"This isn't a weekend retreat to the Canadian

Rockies - we're running away together - just you and me."

"I know that. But apart from the clothes you got me, everything else I own looks only suitable for the garbage."

"Well whatever you've got, just toss it in a bag. Honestly, with what we've now got, you can buy a whole new wardrobe. Listen now, I'll pick you up tomorrow night, eight o'clock sharp."

"Why so late?"

"Well, it is my last day at the hostel tomorrow, and Gerard has been sniffin' around wantin' me to go back to his place. He's promising some bullshit romantic affair, and considering what we're pulling, it'd only raise suspicion if I were to refuse."

"Are you sure he isn't just waiting for you to trip up? How do we know he hasn't been back already?" Davina remarked.

"We don't know ... but if we lose our nerve now, we're as good as dead. This way, both of us will have a fighting chance of coming out of this laughing."

"I don't know. It's all sounds so crazy - why do you want to risk so much for me, Cameron? You and I both know we're only prolonging the inevitable."

Cameron sighed, "Don't you get it yet you stupid girl? I'm in love with you. If I can make whatever time you have left as good as it can possibly be, then God-dammit that's what I'm going to do!"

"Alright, alright. Are you in work now?" Davina asked.

"No, they let me have the afternoon off, so I'm taking the time to get prepared."

"Well, I'm going to have a lie down now. I ain't feeling so good. But don't worry, I'm determined that I will know when my time's up. So, I'll see you tomorrow, yeah?" Davina replied.

Cameron gave a smile of sympathy, "I promise you. Bye now, Davina."

She switched the phone off, laying it on her lap as she felt an overwhelming feeling of sorrow engulf her. Her head was racing, a multitude of thoughts fighting for attention. She closed her eyes.

Out in the hallway, an energetically happy Patricia came to her little sister's door and tried the handle. But the door for some reason was locked. Inside, a tearful Cameron quickly got up from the bed and hid her suitcase underneath and out of sight before yelling: 'Just a minute!'

In the hallway, Patricia waited patiently until she heard the door unlock, then Cameron peered out, looking flushed.

"Cameron, guess what... Julia just said that I... hang on, have you been crying??" Patricia then said, alarmed.

Cameron turned away, rubbing at her eyes with

the back of her hand, then returned to the bed, and straightened the duvet, more to appear busy than anything else.

"Erm, no, I'm... I'm fine, er, I was just thinking about Grandpa. It's the anniversary of his death on Saturday, right?"

Patricia frowned, "And you got upset over that? You never really bothered with Grandpa when he was alive. What gives?"

"Oh you know, I may not have spoken with him much, but I did -"

She already realised her story sounded foolish.

"This is bullshit." Patricia then snapped, "What were you doing, were you on the phone to Davina again? Believe me, it's a waste of time shedding tears over that woman."

Cameron looked at Patricia like she had just stuck a knife in her, "Take that back! You don't know nothing. Davina means everything to me!!" She blurted.

"Oh, it's all coming out now, isn't it? Believe me; if she's capable of sleeping with me behind your back, then she's capable of much more."

"Fuck you, Patricia! You have no right!"

Patricia took a deep breath, then exhaled slowly, realising she'd said too much.

"How has she upset you then?" She asked with sincerity.

"She hasn't." Cameron replied quietly, and sat

down on the end of the bed.

Patricia walked in front of her.

"Then why were you crying?"

"It's really none of your business!"

Patricia looked frustrated, "Well as long as you know what you're doing. We've both hurt you enough to last a life time. I don't want to see you go through anything like that again, that's all." She said, and then returned to the door.

As she went to leave, Cameron looked over to her, tempted to say more but decided not to and Patricia exited the room, leaving the door ajar. With solitude restored, Cameron buried her head in her hands and burst into tears.

*

That night, Gerard Jones stood in the hallway of his apartment, speaking on the phone.

"I understand all that, Mr Leone, but trust me, Don Salvatore has no worries on that part. I'm going to be collecting the money in a little while, and I'll meet you at the place we agreed by ten."

Gerard then switched the phone off and returned it to its charging dock located on a small table next to a bookcase. He walked into the bedroom, and immediately went over to the cupboard beside the bed, kneeling down and feeling with his hand underneath. After a few seconds he retrieved the crumpled map, and as he picked it up, something shiny caught his eye. He then discovered a thin golden ring on the carpet, and grabbed it between finger and thumb, examining it with curiosity. Thinking nothing more; he placed the ring in his pocket and walked out of the room.

At that time, at the Hotel where Malcolm was staying with Jeanie, Cameron walked into the reception, and approached the desk. A man in his early fifties stood to welcome her, and she returned a pretty smile.

"My brother is expecting me, sir - Malcolm Willis." She said, clutching a satchel over her shoulder.

"I see Miss, I'll just telephone his room to check; just formality you understand." the manager replied.

Up in the Hotel room, Malcolm came out of a room putting a black tie on over a dark red shirt, and the intercom buzzed loudly. He approached where it was fixed to the wall next to the door, then pressed a button.

"Willis here; what can I do you for, Mr Moore?" He said.

"A young lady is here, claiming to be your sister - shall I send her right up?" came the manager's voice.

Malcolm frowned, "Yeah... go ahead." He replied.

The manager looked to Cameron and smiled.

"Just take the elevator up to floor nineteen. His is room -"

"451, yeah I know." Cameron interrupted, then walked away, the manager's eyes lingering on her until a young couple reached the desk.

A short while later, Malcolm opened the door to see his kid sister standing in the corridor, admiring the Hotel's extravagant decor.

"What are you doing here? You can't stop long; Jeanie and I are heading out."

"Oh yeah? Where you going?" Cameron replied, walking in as Malcolm stepped aside.

"Oh, just some place downtown - er, you still haven't answered my question."

"Is it a crime to come visit my bro? Patricia and I haven't seen or spoken to you in more than a week."

"Well that ain't technically true - I spoke to Patricia on Saturday." Malcolm added in his defence, "Erm, she said a few things, is she OK?"

"Who, Patricia? Oh yeah, her usual pain-in-the-ass self. Why, what did you two speak about?"

"Oh nothing for you to worry about. So, er, do you want some Orange Juice? I think I've got some in the refrigerator."

"Orange juice? When are you gonna stop treating me like a kid? I'm 23. I'll have a beer if you've got one!" Cameron snapped.

Malcolm walked away, "Erm, there ain't no beer."

"What? Malcolm Willis without alcohol in the place - I don't believe it." Cameron added sarcastically.

"Well that's tough. Just handle it. It's OJ or nothing." Malcolm retorted.

"Whatever." Cameron replied as her brother walked into the kitchen, and she herself lingered in the hallway.

As she stood there, she glanced around, then discovered an assortment of coats hung on a coat stand. Without hesitation, she rushed over, and began to search the pockets, before eventually retrieving a set of keys. She looked through them slowly, then found one that had an engraving that read: 'Lock Up 590 - Marlboro Street'. Smiling on finding exactly what she had come for, she separated the key from the rest with a twist of her hand, then concealed it in her Dungarees.

"You going to drink it standing there, or you gonna come and sit down?" He asked on returning with her OJ, and Cameron moved from the coat rack, hiding the bunch of keys behind her back with a distracting smile.

She then picked her satchel up from where she had dropped it on searching the coats, then hurried after him, placing the keys on a table beside the wall on the way. In the living room, she sat herself down on a leather sofa, and Malcolm looked at her sternly.

"So come on, Cameron, why you really here?" He asked, then sat down in an armchair, with a small coffee table between them.

Malcolm stared at Cameron with fascination as she leaned forward and picked up her glass, then sipped it slowly. He had always had trouble figuring out his kid sister's complex personality, as unlike Patricia, she wasn't so easy to guess. Patricia was like Cameron in the way they could always find themselves making stupid mistakes, but with Cameron, he never saw it coming. This occasion was no different.

CHAPTER 13

That night, a black van arrived outside the cemetery in East LA. The engine ceased, and Gerard climbed out, dressed all in black with a woollen hat over his head. He carried a pair of bolt cutters with him as he approached the tall iron gates.

Once inside, he was unknowingly re-treading Cameron & Davina's footsteps, until eventually he slowed his pace, and came to the unmarked grave. With the map held in his hand, he stood still as a light wind made the crumpled piece of paper flap - then suddenly started to panic.

"Fuck me, this ain't happenin'." He remarked, reading and re-reading the map over and over as he stood before a sectioned off area of the cemetery, bright yellow hazard tape flapping in the wind.

Gerard stepped over the taped off area then stood before a sheet of tarpaulin. Quickly he pulled it away to expose a hole sinking six feet down, and visible at the bottom was a coffin; its lid removed and nothing inside.

"Fuck!" He cursed.

In a small cabin over by a boarded-up church, a door creaked open, and the same ageing Security Guard from the other night peered out. He was able to see Gerard several metres ahead.

"Not again. Damn bastards." He remarked, and turned back to a table where his shotgun was situated. In the subdued lamp light, a plaster was visible above his brow. Grabbing the weapon with shaky hands, he popped the barrel, then loaded two fresh shells, one after the other.

Returning to the door, he opened it slowly, and stepped outside. It was dark, the moonlight disappearing behind the clouds, and he switched his torch on. Then he reached the taped off area, and quickly looked around himself. He was once again alone in the cemetery.

Gerard returned to his van moments later, and paused before climbing in. His mind was racing. He was sure he had the location exact. This was bad. He then reached into the pocket of his trousers, suddenly thinking of that gold ring he found. On raising that same ring before his face, its plated gold glinting in the light from a street lap - his eyes widened with sudden realisation.

"You gotta be kidding me!" He cursed, recognising the ring as the same one that used to pierce

Cameron's lip ... but had been strangely absent of late.

*

Over an hour later, Gerard arrived at an old, abandoned warehouse, and the van's headlights lit up two black cars, where men in black suits stood. Switching off the engine, he climbed out with some unease as he saw Mr Leone approach.

"I hope the money is in the van, Mr Jones, or we will have a situation." He said loudly.

"Erm, well, there's sort of been a problem, Mr Leone, but... just listen to me."

Two huge men in suits then appeared behind Gerard, and Mr Leone stood with his hands behind his back.

"Excuse me? Do I hear an excuse coming here? You know how I feel about excuses Mr Jones." He said.

Gerard glanced around himself and quickly felt ill.

"I went for the money, Mr Leone, you gotta believe me. I've always been on the level with you. Thing is though, it's been lifted. But, but... don't worry, cuz I know who did it, and believe me, she's going to be fuckin' sorry."

"She? You're telling me some dumb broad has ripped you off, and therefore ripped Salvatore off in the process?"

Gerard stared at him fearfully.

"But she don't know I know, Mr Leone. But I'll sort it, you 'ave my fuckin' word!" He explained desperately.

Mr Leone smiled, then glanced to one of the black-suited men. Suddenly Gerard's legs were swiped out from under him as the man to his right swung a Baseball bat, and Gerard fell to the ground with a scream of agony. Mr Leone then began to walk away.

"We'll speak soon, Mr Jones - and let this be a reminder - next time, my boys here may not be so hospitable." He concluded, returning to one of the cars, just as Gerard received another blow.

(Friday)

The following day, Cameron was working in the laundry at the Hostel, folding sheets as Gerard walked in. He stood looking at her and removed a cigarette from his mouth.

"Wanna smoke, darlin'?" He asked, propping himself against a washing machine.

"I've got my own, thank you." She replied, not looking at him.

He scrutinised her like a soldier looking at his enemy, then lit his cigarette on a Zippo, exhaling a cloud of smoke.

"Last day today then. I'll miss you 'round here, you

know."

Cameron suddenly looked at him.

"What are you talkin' about? Our arrangement is still on even after I leave here, isn't it?"

"Well, that's what puzzles me. You don't act like a junkie, and your arms never have any needle marks. You're not supposed to snort that stuff, you know."

"Give me some credit, Gerard. Haven't you ever heard of injecting it between the toes? It's easier to hide, and anyway it's a longer high. You should try it." She said, quoting dialogue from a movie she'd seen.

"Well, yeah ... I guess I will." He replied, then took another drag on his cigarette, grimacing as his ribs pained him.

Cameron then placed some folded sheets on a shelf and went to walk past him, until he grabbed her arm and looked at her sternly. She returned a look of shock, and then he grinned.

"We're gonna set our worlds on fire tonight, sweet 'art." He said.

Cameron smiled back as he released his grip, then walked out as his stare lingered, watching as she proceeded down the corridor.

"Trust me darlin' - your world is going to be blazin'..." He said under his breath, then took another drag of his cigarette.

*

A telephone rang out in the downstairs hallway of the Willis mansion, and Patricia hurried out of a doorway, her hair all wet, wearing an all-in-one swim suit.

"Hello?" She said on lifting the receiver.

"Patricia? It's Malcolm. I tried calling that cell phone I got you, but you've got it switched off."

"Oh yeah, I'm sorry, Mom & Dad are out, Cameron's at the Hostel, and I've got the place to myself, so I thought I'd chill for a few hours by the pool, have a swim, that kind of thing." Patricia enthused.

"So I take it you got your dressing off today, by your good mood."

"Well, yesterday afternoon actually. Er, so what you callin' for?"

"I dunno. Cameron turned up here out of the blue yesterday - did you know anything about that?"

"She came to the Hotel?"

"Yeah."

"Oh right. No, she said nothing to me. Why, did she stay long?"

"Only about a quarter of an hour. She wasn't acting right at all - you don't know if anything's up with her, do you?"

Patricia took a moment to think. She knew if

she told Malcolm what she knew, about Cameron being with Davina again, he'd just go crazy.

"No, I don't know anything. She has been a bit secretive, locking her bedroom door an' all, but as far as telling me - you can forget it. She says she has forgiven me, but I know she's still got a problem whenever I'm around her."

"OK, OK, I'll have to work it out for myself. What about you? Can I rest assured you ain't somebody I need to worry about also?" Malcolm added.

Patricia smiled, appreciating his concern.

"No, I'm OK; I was just feeling nostalgic the other day. But I'm fine now. I'm more interested in you - how's this new business venture working out, and when are you going to let me in on it?"

"I'm not keeping anything from you, sis. I should probably explain more to you in person. But for now, let's just say, a few small ambitions of mine are finally being realised."

"Well, whatever it is, Malcolm, I'm happy for you."

"Thank you, I appreciate that, Patricia. I'll let you get back to your swim now, yeah?"

"I guess. Speak to you soon."

"That's a promise. Bye."

"Bye." Patricia concluded, then hung up, walking away with a silly smile on her face. What did she have to worry about, when she had both her parents, and especially, a wonderful big brother looking out for her? At that moment, she felt more secure in her life than she had ever felt.

* *

That evening, a lock turned in the front door of Gerard Jones' apartment, and the door swung open. Gerard entered slowly, and switched the hallway light on.

"So what's this surprise, Gerard? The anticipation's killin' me." Cameron said, following him inside then closed the door again.

"Interesting choice of words." Gerard replied under his breath, then looked back to her just as she turned to smile at him.

Suddenly, he swung a clenched fist into her face, and she collided against the door with a sharp cry, clutching her nose as it spurted blood. Gerard took another look at her, then punched her again, this time impacting the back of her head with the door, and she slowly slid to the floor, unconscious.

"You stupid, fuckin' bitch. Think you're really smart, don't you? Now look what you made me do!" He exclaimed with aggression, casting his shadow over her.

A short while later, Cameron began to come round, and as she opened her eyes, her vision was blurred and her head pulsed. She felt suddenly euphoric, like she had dropped Acid, but her body was incredibly weak, discovering she could hardly move her arms or legs.

"So you're finally awake?" echoed an unrecognisable voice, her hearing all weird and distorted.

Gerard stood beside the bed where a drip stood on a steel pole feeding a tube taped to Cameron's arm, as she lay stripped down to her underwear, one hand cuffed to the headboard, the other cuffed to the bed frame He sat down, and she moaned an attempt at replying to his voice. Elvis Presley's Always On My Mind played in the background, its very presence ironic.

"Don't try and struggle, darlin'. I've got you being drip-fed Amobarbitol every few minutes. They used to use it in World War Two apparently. But don't worry, it's only enough so I can finally get some answers." He explained calmly.

Cameron sniggered, too whacked out to find the situation anything but amusing.

"What's wrong, you mad at me daddy?" She asked, then sniggered, her nose crimson with dried blood blocking her airway, so she had to breathe through her mouth.

Gerard smiled, and ran a hand up her leg. He could see that her whole body perspired, shining appealingly in the subdued light.

"At one stage, I really did have a nice evening planned for us, you know? I was even gonna give you all that scented candles bullshit with the flower petals in the bathtub. But then some information fell into my lap."

He got up, and paced the floor at the end of the bed.

"So, answer me this. How long was this whole thing planned? Did you find my map, is that it?"

"You weren't exactly hidin' it in a secret special place, were you?" Cameron replied, looking wide eyed around the room.

"OK, that was my mistake. I stupidly trusted you. I suppose I can't blame you though, I haven't exactly treated you the best. But I'm sorry about that. Yet doing this to me, it's going too far. Where have you got the money? I know you have it, 'cause I've been back to the cemetery, and I'm afraid the cupboard was bare."

"Ooh, that would be telling now, wouldn't it?" Cameron replied playfully.

Gerard sighed, "What I don't understand, is how you pulled it off. Did you do this all on your own, dig the grave up and everything? It just doesn't ring true. Was there a third party involved? Is this anything to do with that asshole brother of yours?"

Cameron grinned, "It's nothing to do with him. He couldn't bluff his way out of a nose-picking contest. No, that was my sweet pea, that was Davina." She replied, giving little regard to what she was saying or who she was saying it to.

"Davina?" Gerard retorted with confusion, "Why does that name ring a bell?"

"Oh you remember, Davina, don't you? Sure you do. She used to get her drugs off you, until she got into debt and you had her hospitalised that one time."

Gerard frowned, "Cheeky bitch." He remarked, and pictured his old client for a moment, "Fuckin' cheeky bitch."

"So where am I, is this a holiday, are we on honeymoon?" Cameron then asked, and she examined the ceiling and walls, unable to recognise them in her state of bewilderment.

Gerard stared at her, and the drip bubbled, feeding more drugs into Cameron's blood stream.

"OK. I need an address. If you're not going to tell me where the doe is, I think that cunt of a friend might."

Cameron tugged at the cuffs fixing her hand to the headboard, and screwed her face up, "Oh, I can't rub my nose. I don't like this game." She remarked with child-like frustration.

"Later, treacle - just tell me where she is, and all this nasty business can be put behind us."

"Well, if I wasn't so sleepy, I'd draw you a map, but instead I'll just tell you. She lives in an apartment building on Penbury Drive. Do you know where that is? It's only half an hour's drive from the Hostel. It's a bit run down, hasn't seen a decorator in years. I'd give it a woman's touch but you see, I really haven't the time these days."

Gerard smiled and walked back to the bed side, leaning close to Cameron.

"I knew you'd come through darlin'." He remarked, then backed off to the bedroom door, "I've just gotta go out now. Don't go anywhere, will ya?" He added, sniggering mischievously before exiting the room, leaving the door open to light Cameron up as she groaned and closed her eyes.

CHAPTER 14

Davina stood in the graffiti covered corridor of her apartment building, having been talking to a neighbour, "Oh come on Bobby. You telling me you're all out? That's just bullshit." She said with a raised voice, then the apartment door was slammed in her face.

Stepping back, she kicked the door with frustration, then wandered back to her own door which stood ajar. Inside she walked up the hallway, rubbing her arm where track marks disfigured her skin, the usual aches and cramps filling her body from head to toe. On entering her bathroom, she picked up a used needle from the wash basin, then discarded it into a wastepaper basket, and opened her medicine cabinet, which it turned out only housed a single packet of sanitary towels and some paracetamol. She sighed, closing the cabinet again. For a moment she examined her reflection. She looked even paler than usual she thought, as she stood wearing a dirty grey sleeveless vest and sweatpants.

Just then everything went pitch black as her hallway light went off, making her turn around in alarm. Silence lingered for a moment until all she heard was a floorboard creak. As she waited the continuing darkness was enough to build her fear. Finally she stepped forward, reaching out with one hand and felt for a light switch. Suddenly, the bathroom light came on, and she cried out on coming face to face with her intruder, a very stern looking Gerard Jones.

"Allo, darlin'." He said with an evil grin, then grabbed her by her face, yanking her out of the room, and she hit the wall hard.

Still feeling the effects from her cramps, she looked around with confusion, until a swipe to the face with the back of Gerard's hand caused her to drop to the floor.

"You stupid Dyke slut!" He exclaimed, "Tell me where my money is, or I'll fuckin' end you!"

Davina began to crawl away on hands and knees, and her bedroom door came into view just feet from where she was situated.

"Where you goin'? There's no escaping now, you stupid bitch! Tell me what I want to know, or I'll fuck you up real bad!!"

Davina crawled to her feet, supporting herself against the wall, then glanced back, feeling punch-drunk. For the first time, she suddenly realised who she was looking at, and a cold pulse shot through her body. If Gerard was here, she thought to herself - then what had he done to Cameron?

"You haven't hurt her, have you?" She asked, backing off.

Gerard approached purposely slow, then opened his long leather trench coat to reveal an iron crowbar. Davina's eyes widened in response.

"You shouldn't be thinkin' about Cameron right now, you should be focusing on gettin' me my money, is that clear?" He replied, calmly threatening.

"It's, it's in the bedroom, I swear! Erm, let me get it for you, yeah?" Davina replied nervously, then turned and grabbed the handle of the bedroom door, pushing it open.

Gerard then rushed after her, "Hey, not so fast, darlin'." He said.

Davina paused in the door way, her back to him. As she stood there, she touched the door with her hand, then ran her fingers up it, before curling her arm around to feel for a coat hanging up on the other side.

"What's the problem?" She asked, "Do you want your money or not?"

Then she looked back to Gerard just as the coat inside the room fell from its hanger, and she managed to grab it with her hand, then slowly went about searching it, twisting the coat around, until she felt a bulge in the inside pocket.

Suddenly, Gerard grabbed her, pulling her away from the door, just as the coat fell to the floor. Then Davina turned to face Gerard, pointing the Security Guard's Revolver into his chest.

"Away, now!" She exclaimed, and cocked the hammer back.

Gerard noticed the gun, and backed off.

"Smart move, darlin' - didn't see that one coming." He said, and stepped away to the wall, suddenly colliding with a table, and the telephone fell off, making a loud bell-like noise on impact with the floor.

Gerard jolted in reaction and turned to look, then as Davina approached him, he suddenly swung the crowbar and hit her across the face, knocking her back into the room, and she tripped and fell. A loud bang rang out as the Revolver went off, and Gerard screamed in agony as he was blasted in the knee cap. He slid to the floor in pain. Davina lay half in and half out of her bedroom, the Revolver still clutched in her hand, smoke rising into the air above. Raising her head to see what had happened, she then gasped on seeing Gerard, slumped over and crying like a baby.

"Ooh shit, sorry about that, man." She remarked, then sat up before getting to her feet again.

Gerard looked at her and sighed. Davina's face echoed the pity she felt, and the gun was cocked back for a second time.

"Tell me where she is."

"Go fuck yourself!" Gerard snapped in response.

She aimed the gun at his head.

"It makes no difference to me, whether you live or die; now tell me where the fuck you've got Cameron! She was going back to your place tonight. The address, now!!"

Gerard just stared at her, as he lay in a thick pool of blood and his knee shot razor-sharp pain through the lower half of his body.

"Then you'll just have to kill me." He breathed.

A few seconds passed by. Davina then lowered the gun, reaching down to pick up the crowbar from where it lay beside Gerard.

"I might be many things ... but I ain't no killer." She replied, and suddenly swung the crowbar, knocking Gerard out cold.

Soon, Davina, a bruise having swollen her bottom lip, and a cut above her brow, sat in the driver's seat of Gerard's black van, thumbing through the $20 bills lining his wallet, then removed an I.D. card. It detailed his address, along with a photograph. Smirking to herself, she started the engine with Gerard's lifted keys.

"You've still got it, girl." She commented, then saw the van's headlights illuminate the rest of the road outside the run-down apartment building she had called home for far longer than she'd ever intended.

She was finally turning her back on it though - but hopefully hadn't left it too late.

*

Back at Gerard's apartment, little under an hour later, Cameron was in semi-slumber, her body tingling, and images from throughout her young life flashed in her head. She recalled first confessing her sexuality to Patricia whilst sitting on swings at a park they had frequented as kids. Then her first sexual encounter with Davina in that crappy camper van, an environment masked by the passionate recoil of emotions and physical need that she never forgot. She knew it could never be like that again, yet to still have Davina in her life was all that mattered now.

The door opened in the hallway, and Davina rushed in, "Cameron?" She called with desperation, "Shit babe, where are you?"

Cameron's eyes sprung open on hearing Davina's voice, followed by the bedroom door creaking, and then a shadow was cast over her.

"Oh my god, Cameron - what has that scumbag done to you??" Davina exclaimed, hurrying to the bedside and looking at her friend like she in-fact was the one dying, and not herself.

"Fuckin' psycho bastard." She remarked, then found a small key on the bedside table, and was quick to unfasten the handcuffs securing Cameron to the bed.

"We gotta get this thing out of you babe, shit - what's he fuckin' feeding you??" She asked.

"I'm floating." Cameron then said with a weak, croaky voice.

"OK, I've got it now - now hold on, this might sting." Davina replied, as she held Cameron's hand then removed the tube that hooked her up to the drip.

Cameron didn't batter an eye lid as it was removed, clearly too far gone to react much to pain.

"Right - let's get you dressed and the fuck out of here." Davina added, and called on the limited strength she still had, to pull Cameron from the bed, and carry, half dragging her out of the room.

In the living room, she let Cameron slump in Gerard's armchair, then returned to the bedroom to grab her clothes and anything else of her friend's she could find.

A few minutes later they proceeded down the corridor, with Davina holding a fully dressed Cameron around the waist, preventing her from falling over, as she mumbled and spoke nonsensical. Eventually they reached an elevator, and Davina propped Cameron against the wall as she hit the call button.

"How you doin', girl?" She asked.

"I feel funny - I think I'm gonna puke."

"Well, I think you'll be OK, he didn't have that thing hooked up so you'd O.D. But it might take a few hours for it to vacate your system. Crazy fuckin' bastard. Hey, if you're going to puke, go right ahead."

Cameron nodded, then jerked forward and vomited onto the floor, gasping for breath and groaning.

Davina allowed Cameron to sleep it off in the back of the van as she herself drove. As the van travelled out of town, Davina tuned the radio, and some rock music came on to soothe the aches and pains in her body. She was not really in a fit state to drive, but in comparison, was far more suited to the task than Cameron.

As it turned One a.m. the van arrived outside a series of garages on a secluded stretch of road. Cameron was now sitting looking wrecked in the passenger seat; her complexion ghostly, hair messy despite the braiding, and like Davina, bruises covered her face, where Gerard had left his mark.

"So you're sure this is the place?" Davina asked.

"Yeah." Cameron replied quietly, then routed inside her satchel, "This is all I've got? I really wished my suitcase with me ... but I suppose I never figured how I was meant sneak it from the house." She remarked, before retrieving a small key with an engraving that read: 'Lock up 590, Marlboro Street'.

"Well I wouldn't worry too much, babe... it's like you said, with the money we now have, getting new threads won't be a problem." Davina replied optimistically, "So... are we gonna crack this baby open or what?"

Cameron perked up and opened the door, climbing out, and her legs felt like jelly as she walked over to the lock-up. Davina followed after her, carrying Gerard's crowbar, until they reached a garage, and Cameron unlocked the doors with the stolen key.

"You alright to start it up?" She asked, then raised the vertical door to reveal the inside of the garage, where two distinctively beautiful cars were stored; a blood-red Lotus Esprit and a black Porsche 911.

"You've got some style, kid. I'll give you that." Davina remarked appreciatively, then walked over to the Porsche, and tried the door - it was locked.

"I don't suppose you got the keys to this, have you?" She asked.

"I can't supply everything, Davina - you're supposed to be the car-jacking expert 'round here."

Davina smiled, then applied the crowbar to the car-door, a shatter of glass piercing the night like a scream.

"I wasn't really talkin' about you fuckin' wrecking it!" Cameron exclaimed.

"Well, with these tools, a girl's gotta improvise - now get your stuff and let's book."

Cameron sighed, walking back to the van and proceeding to the passenger side to grab her satchel, along with a pack of cigarettes and her baseball cap. Closing the door, she looked back to the garage as the Porsche rolled out, the hum of its engine making the ground vibrate beneath her feet. She grinned then rushed over, jumping into the passenger side. Davina then stamped on the accelerator - and almost as quickly as they had arrived, they were gone.

CHAPTER 15

(Saturday)

Patricia rolled onto her back in bed at the Willis mansion, and opened her eyes to the sound of voices coming from the next room. Slowly sitting up, she pulled the covers away, then climbed out. She walked across the length of her pastel-pink room, grabbing a dressing gown on her way, putting it on over simple, silk underwear. For a moment she noticed herself in a full-length mirror next to an antique wardrobe.

Out in the corridor seconds later, Patricia approached Cameron's room, and heard the familiar sound of her mother, Barbara talking inside. *Had Cameron come home?* Patricia asked herself. They had all been so concerned when she didn't turn up at all the previous night. Quickly, Patricia grabbed the handle and pushed the inwards, then was presented with the sight of both her parents, standing before Cameron's bed, and they turned to see her as she entered.

"Patricia..." Edward announced as if surprised by her intrusion, and Barbara and himself parted to reveal an opened, packed suitcase on the bed.

"What's going on?? Cameron not come home??" Patricia exclaimed with concern.

Barbara rubbed a hand across her mouth, and sighed, "No dear, and we've just found this. I-I er... don't know what's got into her lately, but it seems like your sister was planning a trip, maybe even running away."

"Nonsense!" Patricia replied with disbelief.

"It sure does look that way, dear, her drawers are all empty. She's packed like she wasn't planning on coming back anytime soon." Edward remarked.

"Then why hasn't she taken her suitcase?"

"We're not sure, honey, er, it doesn't make a lot of sense." Barbara said with a concerned yet puzzled expression.

Patricia turned away, "I've gotta make a phone call." She said then walked back down the corridor.

She re-entered her room and returned to the bed, sitting down on the patterned duvet, then picked up her cell from a bedside cabinet.

Inside a traveling Limo, Mr Leone reacted to a phone ringing, and revealed a cell from inside his suit jacket.

"Hello?" He said as he held it to his ear, "Ahh Mr Jones - I presume you phoning me today is to bring me good news..."

Back at Davina's apartment, a very pale Gerard was on the floor in the hallway, propped against the wall, the receiver of Davina's telephone held to his ear. His blasted kneecap was awash with blood, and a crimson puddle covered the floor all around him.

"Not exactly Mr Leone, but don't erm, don't be worrying, it's only a minor setback." He said, considerably weakened.

Mr Leone glanced to a younger Italian beside him, then continued talking, "I'd really rather not hear about setbacks, Mr Jones. This is fuckin' unacceptable. You just tell me this girl's name, and I'll have someone professional settle this matter once and for all."

"My thoughts exactly - but first we need to find them. Her and that dyke friend of hers; some junkie, have gone and done a runner. They could be anywhere by now."

"This isn't exactly cheering me up, Mr Jones."

"Yes, but listen ... I've got an idea that I think you just might like." Gerard replied, as he held up a strip of photo-booth pictures, showing Cameron

& Davina huddled together, taken only recently going by both girls' newly obtained haircuts.

*

A little while later, Malcolm's Merc' arrived outside a run-down apartment building, and Patricia glanced out of the window.

"Are you sure this is the place, sis? It looks ready to be knocked down." Malcolm remarked.

"Yeah this is it – Davina and I used to come back here sometimes when we had nowhere else to go."

"Why couldn't you have just told me about Davina before all of this? Maybe I could have spoken to Cameron, helped her in some way."

"I doubt it, Malcolm. I tried to warn her off Davina myself. I know she's bad news - I guess that was part of the initial attraction - but, I dunno, I also didn't want to complicate things any further between Cameron and myself, more than they already are."

Malcolm switched off the engine, "Well, whatever she's got herself into now, we won't solve anything sitting here reminiscing over bad decisions - let's go inside."

Patricia unclipped her seat belt then opened the door, wearing a Denim skirt with knee-length boots and a loose-fitting shirt, as a mid-morning breeze made the hem flap around her waist.

Soon they stood in an elevator that smelt badly of urine and was covered in graffiti. Malcolm was dressed casually in a tight black T-shirt and Levis, the Rolex on his wrist glinted in the glow from a flickering strip light above.

"Oh Jesus, look..." Patricia remarked, careful not to step in bloody boot prints and several spots of blood on the elevator floor.

"Looks fresh." Malcolm added, then produced a revolver from where it had been stuffed in the back of his jeans.

"Malcolm! What's that for?!" Patricia exclaimed.

"Just leave this to me, sis." He replied, cold and calculated.

Patricia just looked away.

The elevator stopped at the third floor, and Patricia instinctively backed away as Malcolm rolled back the iron gate, then paused.

"What you waiting for?" Patricia asked.

"Check this out." Malcolm replied, and Patricia stepped forward to see a trail of blood leading directly from the elevator.

She placed a hand over her mouth, horrified.

"D-Does it go all the way down the corridor?" Patricia asked on lowering her hand, and walked cautiously out of the elevator.

Malcolm looked back to her, then followed her the

other way, until they reached an open apartment.

"This is Davina's. Oh God..." Patricia commented.

"Step aside, sis." Malcolm said, then pointed the Revolver, entering the apartment hallway.

The trail of blood stopped at a thicker pool of blood and further boot prints located beside a table. A telephone sat on the floor, its receiver buzzing a dial tone.

"Someone's been here, that's for sure." He said, and looked around, then knelt down to pick up an empty bullet casing.

"Interesting." He commented, then walked into the living room, and a smell hit his nostrils as he discovered a half-eaten take-away on the coffee table amongst cans of Lager and an overflowing ashtray.

"It's alright, Patricia - I don't think anyone's here now." He called, and within seconds, Patricia appeared behind him.

"Jesus Christ, this place is a dump." She said with surprise, glancing over Malcolm's shoulder.

He turned and walked back into the hallway, and entered the bedroom. The bed was neatly made, but clothes littered the floor. He went back out and entered the bathroom, and stale smell lingering in the air.

"This is repugnant." He remarked in a whisper.

Patricia then entered the bedroom, and as she focused on Davina's bed, an image flashed in her mind. She held her breath and stepped back on seeing herself writhing under the covers with Davina, the two of them making love in a way Patricia had never managed to better with any other lover.

She closed her eyes momentarily, then flinched at the sound of Malcolm's voice.

"Patricia? Where are you?" He asked as he came back into the hallway, then reached down and replaced the buzzing telephone receiver back in its cradle.

Patricia left the bedroom, and Malcolm turned to look at her, just as she caught a tear of reminiscence with her finger as it escaped her eye lid.

"You alright?" He asked.

She breathed in, swallowing her emotions, then sighed. She returned a nod, then passed him, proceeding to the door.

"Let's go Malcolm." She said solemnly.

Malcolm frowned, "So er, what do you make of all this?" He asked.

"Let's just go back to the car - I can't handle this right now."

"Are you serious? We've got a situation here, sis!"

Patricia looked back to him, and her eyes glistened wet, "I don't know what Cameron & Davina are involved in," She then exclaimed, "but I'm sure if either of them were hurt, or even dead, if this blood was theirs, I'd know - I can't explain how, but I'd definitely know. Is that good enough for you?"

Malcolm saw the look in her eyes, and realised pressing the matter any further would be unwise. He put the revolver away in the back of his jeans, then followed her out, careful to avoid the blood as they headed back to the elevator.

CHAPTER 16

The Affair

Four years ago…

It was the evening after Patricia had graduated from university. She had done well, coming away with a degree in law. When she returned home, she had been expecting some sort of celebration, however her parents this time had gone all out. Their perfect, butter wouldn't melt favourite child had done good. Rarely had such adoration been bestowed on her other siblings, going some way to explaining their more rebellious attitudes to family life.

It was seven o'clock when she returned home to the party after a few drinks out with her boyfriend of several years, beach-bum surfer James Burrows. The two had been in and out of love since high school, and he also happened to be Malcolm's best friend. Champagne was popped open. Patricia was greeted with hugs & kisses from Barbara & Edward, and there was a table ten foot long full of the finest food money could buy. She was impressed by the music as well, not too loud - after all, she hadn't saved the world or something, just been away for twelve months, studying hard and supporting herself on her father's credit cards. Yes, life was easy in the Willis household, or at least, that is what everyone would have had you believe.

The truth was, her mother didn't really get on with her father; Edward being so set in his ways and very strict. Patricia loved the both of them very much, but whether they thought that of each other was up for debate. Then there were the kids. Malcolm back then was 28, already a bit of a player, a ladies man and occasional gambler. Around that time, he had run up debts with the local crime syndicates that ran all the casinos from LA to Las Vegas, and was also suspected of being involved in more than a few questionable deals. Then there was Cameron. Still a slip of a girl at 19, but she had come 'out' as gay when she was sixteen, and Mom & Dad were not in approval. Even worse, she had chosen to bring her current girlfriend 'Davina' to the party ... and it was there that everything began for Patricia.

The party continued for hours; with Barbara & Edward retiring to bed by midnight, and Patricia had been the centre of attention for most of the evening. She had spoken to relatives, young and old, and received gifts from friends old and new, but for the most part, Cameron had kept her mysterious, dark-haired lover to herself. She hadn't even spoken to Patricia much, and Patricia returned a suspicion that Cameron resented the attention.

Patricia had her eye on Davina throughout, getting caught staring several times. Patricia had felt herself blush when Davina smiled back at her. The girl was appealing in a way that couldn't be explained. She hadn't exactly dressed for the occasion, wearing Levis and a black sleeveless vest, the tightness of the fabric making it obvious she wasn't wearing anything underneath. Such disregard for convention made Patricia incredibly attracted to her.

As if to deny her feelings, Patricia disappeared upstairs, and entered a bathroom. Running the water in the washing basin, she freshened up, systematically wiping all the makeup from her face. When she had finished, her reflection surprised her - she looked far prettier without all the eyeliner and mascara. Her sapphire eyes seemed to sparkle. She was proud of how she looked, and had always worn her fair hair shoulder length, sometimes as long as down her back, but never, ever short. Drying her hands on a towel, she then turned to the door, and then gasped as it opened.

Davina entered and focused on Patricia immediately.

"I bet you thought nobody saw you come up here all on your own ..." She remarked.

"Excuse me?" Patricia replied.

"It's alright; I saw the way you were looking at me."

Davina had an arrogance to her words, and was taking charge of the situation. Patricia began to feel powerless, and backed away to the wall.

"What about Cameron?" She asked, although her sister's feelings hadn't really concerned her when she had been so obviously checking Davina out.

"Don't worry about her - nobody else exists right now, only you and me." Davina replied coming up so close to Patricia that she could smell her sweet natural odour.

Then Davina did the unthinkable, she pressed her body against Patricia and clamped her mouth over hers. Patricia's eyes closed, then she felt Davina's hand burrow under her dress and grasp her crotch. A moan escaped Patricia's mouth as they kissed, and Davina's rubbing hand quickly made her wet. Then her hand was inside her knickers, and her fingers were digging into Patricia's vagina. Patricia's pulse increased and she grabbed Davina around the waist, holding her as she was fingered and kissed with a passion she had never previously experienced.

Davina pulled away. Patricia's face was flushed. She relaxed against the wall, and Davina backed off, wiping her mouth on the back of her hand.

"What are you doing?" Patricia then exclaimed, her breath ragged, body trembling.

"Not here." Davina then said, "We'll have to meet somewhere else, tomorrow maybe."

Patricia then stepped forward, and reached her hand out, stroking Davina's hair, "No, don't leave me like this, please!" She begged, her whole body tingling.

Davina looked at her and smiled, putting an arm around her waist, then kissed her gently on the lips. Patricia then responded, and buried her tongue in the dark-haired girl's mouth. Davina pulled away again, gasping.

"No. I'll contact you." She said, then turned away, opened the door, and was gone.

That was how it started, her most illicit of affairs that nobody could ever know about. How would they take it? The golden girl of the family turning out to swing both ways? Yes, she loved James, and she always would, but Davina; well, she was tapping into a part of her that had lay buried for too long. Patricia had always questioned her sexuality, and the answers now flooding her way were far from comfortable. Yet from the moment her and Davina could first be alone together, it also felt so right.

Patricia contorted her face as a fire radiated between her legs. The sensations sweeping through the lower half of her body were unlike anything she had ever experienced. Clutching the bedsheet up to her chin, she struggled and failed not to moan and gyrate, closing her eyes and biting her lip any time it felt too good. Davina's tongue replaced her skilled fingers, slithering slowly across the swell of Patricia's stomach, along the crease of her groin, edging nearer and nearer to the wetness of her vagina.

Patricia gasped and groaned then held her breath as the tongue made contact with her clit, lapping gently as it throbbed, until soft lips closed over it to suck and salivate. Squirming from the many tiny sensations, it was like an energy in her loins, gradually building, flooding her abdomen, making every nerve ending fight for attention. Then the tongue stabbed into her, thrusting rapidly like a little penis, as Davina's hungry mouth clamped down, her hot breath only adding to the pleasure that grew stronger and stronger. Patricia's knuckles turned white as she gripped the sheet tighter, and she began to yelp and gasp as the feelings pushed up through her body, making her nipples sting and her head rush, like her very soul was being forced out of her as she was flung, finally, screaming into orgasm.

Time seemed to stop as sexual gratification

washed over her, then as she began to relax, she grew aware of Davina moving, trailing kisses up her body, until she emerged from under the sheet. Patricia smiled, face flushed and raised her head from the pillow to meet Davina's mouth with a lingering, appreciative kiss.

That wasn't their only encounter. From that seedy hotel room, they went on to have many more secret liaisons. Patricia would meet with Davina whilst on a family holiday where Cameron had brought along her lover, and they would make love at night, by the riverside of the forest where her father owned a private log cabin. They would also regularly meet in similar hotel rooms, and as the weeks passed by, Davina would teach Patricia more about the delights of sex than she could ever have explored with James. Gradually, that relationship would begin to fade as a result, with James noticing a distance within her, and a lack of interest whenever he wanted to fuck her.

Patricia's obsession for Davina grew, and Davina never denied her a thing, answering her and teaching her, until their affair became bolder and more daring. It reached the pinnacle of their infatuation, when Davina came to visit when Patricia was alone in the Bel Air mansion where she had grown up, and still lived with her parents.

Believing they wouldn't be disturbed, they went skinny dipping in the Mansion's in-door swimming pool, drank champagne, chatted for over an hour, reclining on sun-loungers, then concluded with an energetic sex-session on Patricia's bed.

Patricia slept in Davina's arms as the afternoon sun flooded the room from the open window, and the drapes swayed in the breeze. Davina lay awake, lazily stroking Patricia's soft hair and thinking about nothing in particular. It was bliss, sheer bliss, that they both hoped would never end. Davina really began to think she was falling in love with this rich, attractive woman of 24 years of age to her tender 21.

Then without warning, the door swung open, and kid-sister Cameron entered in mid-speech.

"Hey sis, guess what, Malcolm's just picked me up in his new - " then she froze as she saw the two lovers.

Davina stared back at her in silence, then Patricia groaned, her head resting on Davina's breast, and she opened her eyes just as Malcolm joined his sister in the doorway.

"Hey, Cameron, is she in?" He asked, then saw what Cameron was seeing, her mouth open in an all-engulfing sense of shock and betrayal.

"Oh my God, Patricia!" Malcolm then exclaimed, and Cameron turned and ran out, rushing down the staircase like she was being chased.

Patricia sat up in alarm, and pulled the covers

around herself. Malcolm took one look at her, then lurched forward, grabbed Davina violently by her hair, who cried out as he pulled her from the bed, and shoved her into the hallway.

"Get out, you fuckin' bitch, get out!!" He yelled, before slamming the door, leaving him alone to face his sister.

A brief silence lingered. Patricia bowed her head. She couldn't believe what was happening - how could this have happened? How could they have been so reckless?

"How long has this been going on?" He asked demandingly.

Patricia didn't reply, sitting on the bed, feeling vulnerable and ashamed.

"I suppose it explains why you've gone so cold on James. Do you realise what you've done? I'll be very surprised if Cameron ever speaks to you again, and as for that dyke. Well ..."

"Leave her alone." Patricia then said, holding the bed sheets around her to conceal her nudity.

"What was that? You're not telling me you care for that tramp."

Patricia looked at him, "What if I do? You'd never understand."

She got up from the bed and went to pass him, until Malcolm grabbed her violently and thrust her back against the wall. She grunted on impact and stared into his fierce eyes. His fingernails dug into her arms, and she squirmed.

"Malcolm! You're hurting me!"

She saw a hatred and disgust in his eyes that he had never shown before. It frightened her.

"How could you be so stupid? Don't you realise how you'll disappoint Mom & Dad? They think you're better than this!" He then shouted.

And she said back, close to tears, "I was never going to live up to their idea of me, so why try? You and Cameron have done worse things, why is it so different for me?"

Malcolm then let go of her and backed away, then slumped down on the bed, "I don't know." He said with a sigh, "Maybe because you are different. You're better than me or Cameron."

Patricia looked at him as the tears escaped to roll down her cheeks.

"That's it." She said, sniffing loudly, "I've gotta get out of here. I'll take grandfather's inheritance, and just go, never come back."

Malcolm looked at her with concern, "Hey, don't say that, you can't go, I won't let you."

He got up and came up close to her, "You're not thinking straight." He said gently.

Patricia stared at him with wet eyes, "Oh, aren't I?" She replied with defiance.

CHAPTER 17

(Las Vegas, Nevada)

Cameron heard a voice. It called a name. It didn't seem like hers, and yet at the same time, it seemed very much like hers.

"Selena?" the voice came again, a man's voice, "Hey baby, time to wake up."

Her face was the picture of innocent beauty, and her nose wrinkled up as she began to come round. On opening her eyes; framed with glitter make up - Cameron was met with the face of a long-haired ageing man wearing round, red-lensed shades. His aftershave was strong, but the stench of alcohol in the air easily overwhelmed it.

"Johnny? Oh, what time is it?" She asked, yawning.

Johnny moved from the leather sofa where Cameron had crashed out the night before. She was fully dressed in leather and lace like some throwback eighties rock chick.

"It's gone noon, babe - you've been out cold since 12 o'clock last night." Johnny answered.

From his accent, he sounded English, and probably grew up in Liverpool, or there about. He reminded her of old Beatles footage she'd watched as a child. Cameron sat up and brushed her hair back, which was now free of the braiding and back to its regular, lengthy platinum blonde. She felt fresh, rejuvenated, but not relaxed; she could never be relaxed unless she knew where Davina was twenty-four-seven.

"Er... have you seen Caroline?" She asked, using Davina's chosen alias.

"Your friend took off with Andrew earlier on, Selina, probably to see if they could score some more Coke."

"She went off with Andrew? Shit... she never goes anywhere without telling me." Cameron remarked.

"Hey, relax darlin', Andrew's cool - and anyway, I'm sure they'll bring back enough for all of us." Johnny reassured with a kind but simplistic smile.

Cameron quickly got up from the sofa and walked giddily across the Hotel room, "I don't want any fuckin' Coke - I just want my friend!" She snapped, walking to an open door and stepping over discarded clothing, beer cans, and a couple of bongs, before leaving.

It had been three weeks since she had run away with Davina, and as she proceeded down the corridor, not exactly knowing where she was heading - the sound of laughter and mingled voices alerted her. As Cameron neared the end of the corridor, a group of young girls appeared, dressed not dissimilar to herself.

"Selina! You're awake then..." announced one, red-haired girl, swigging a bottle of Champagne as she brushed past Cameron.

"Any of you girls seen ... Caroline?" She asked.

"Caroline?" a Black girl replied, sporting an impressive afro "Yeah, she's down in the lobby with Andrew, why?"

"Oh, nothing." Cameron said, then hurried onwards.

Soon, Cameron walked through a well populated Hotel lobby, where a few celebrities mingled with the general public. But Cameron had no time to put names to faces, as she made a bee-line for Davina.

"Hey, Selina!" Andrew then announced, a bald-headed over-weight man, wearing brightly coloured loose-fitting clothes, who was sitting with Davina beside a fountain.

Davina, who looked near unrecognisable in an eye-catching suede jacket and white jeans combo, seemed peaceful and chilled out, hardly noticing

Cameron as she approached.

"Andrew - you and Caroline been havin' a good time?" Cameron asked, slightly accusing.

Davina opened her eyes, then smirked, "Oops, Mommy's mad with me." She said in a mocking, kindergarten voice.

"We've just been visiting some buddies of mine, that is all babe." Andrew then said in an English accent, "Why don't you head back upstairs, and we'll all cook up a nice little party later on, yeah?"

Cameron stared at an obviously out of it Davina, but despite herself, couldn't help but feel happy seeing her friend looking so well. She knew it was really all down to the alcohol and drugs she'd consumed, keeping her stomach cramps and cold-sweats at bay - but at least Davina seemed happy, and no matter what, Cameron couldn't deny her that.

"OK. Erm, Caroline? I'm stepping out for a little while - gotta get some air. I'll see you later on, alright?" She said to Davina.

Davina didn't look, but gave a thumbs up as if trying to maintain her current buzz, and Cameron walked away as Andrew draped his arm gently over Davina's shoulders.

Cameron left the extravagant towering Hotel in the centre of Las Vegas' famous strip, and stood beside the main road as cars whizzed past, and her hair was blown by the breeze. She felt flustered and overwhelmed. Vegas had that effect on most people, but this wasn't the case with Cameron. The reality was, she was on the run from a psycho drug dealer, and with thousands of dollars of stolen cash in her possession; she had every right to be nervous. She just wished Davina could appear to feel the same. Despite the two of them being in the same mess, Cameron felt like she was the only one experiencing any of it.

A black car with tinted windows drove past Cameron at that moment, and in the back, two well-built, heavily tanned Italian men in their mid to late thirties, sat together, looking through a pile of papers.

"Let me have a look at one of those, Tony." one of the men said, and was then handed a photocopy of the photo-booth picture showing Cameron & Davina, which had been blown up to A4 size.

"Huh. Kinda cute this blonde piece of ass, don't you think, Chrissy?" the other man added.

Tony took a closer look at the photocopy, "I dunno. Blondes are OK for a cheap fuck, but well, this other girl, the brunette - now she's interesting. We'll have to find some time to get better acquainted with these girls before we have to kill 'em." He remarked.

"I'll certainly second that, T." Christopher replied with enthusiasm.

Soon the car arrived outside a small club just off from the main strip, and the two men climbed out, closing the doors, then entered a side alley. Soon they reached a door and pressed a buzzer. They waited patiently, dressed in designer suits, then the door opened to reveal a young Black man.

"Can I help you?" He asked.

"Is your boss in, buddy?" Tony asked.

"Who's asking?"

"Does the name Salvatore Concotti ring any bells? We're associates of his." Christopher then added.

The Black man looked concerned, "Ah right, how's 'bout you gentlemen come in then?" He asked, and stepped aside, allowing the two large Italians entry.

They reached an office minutes later, and the Black man knocked on the door twice.

"Who is it?" came a gruff voice from inside.

"Boss? There are two gentlemen here to see you. They say they're associates of Salvatore..." - the Black man looked to Christopher for confirmation.

"Concotti."

"Yeah, Salvatore Concotti." the guy repeated.

"Excuse me?? Well Lenny, don't stand out there like a fuckin' lemon, show our guests in!" the man's voice replied.

Lenny opened the door and showed Tony & Christopher inside, and they found themselves in a rather untidy office, where a fat, ageing man in a well-worn suit sat behind a desk, pouring himself a Brandy. A poster of a bare breasted model was pinned to a wall directly behind him.

"So, you boys work for Don Salvatore, huh? What brings you to Vegas?" He asked, as Lenny left them alone, closing the door.

Tony stepped forward and placed one of the photocopies on the desk.

The man looked to the photocopy of Cameron & Davina's faces, "Hmm, not bad - what you doin', offering their asses to the highest bidder?" He asked, "I'll tell you now, a lot of trailer-trash bitches pass through this town with dreams of landing a high roller or starring in a show. Most just end up as hookers or dead."

Tony smiled, "Well these girls, they're different - you see, they stole a considerable amount of money from us, and so we're in the process of circulating their picture in case somebody recognises 'em."

"Oh, I see." the man replied, suddenly taking more than a casual interest and picked up the paper as he put on a pair of glasses.

"You know, I think I've seen these two around, but... I'm not as young as I used to be, and I find a cash-incentive can sometimes jog the old brain cells. Do you see where I'm coming from, boys?"

Tony smirked, then glanced to Christopher, who suddenly rushed around the other side of the desk, and pulled the man out of his chair, shoving him violently against a wall, tearing the poster. The man struggled and squirmed, clearly terrified.

Tony's eyes bulged with anger as he shouted, "Forget your fuckin' incentives, pops! You have even the slightest idea where we can locate these cheap-ass-motherfuckin' bitches ... you best be spilling it in our direction, or my friend here will put you in a neck brace for the rest of the year!"

Out in the hallway, Lenny listened against the door, looking increasingly nervous. He placed his hand on a gun tucked into his Levi's.

"OK, OK, just get this goon off me, will yah?" the man then shouted, somewhat shaken.

Christopher relinquished his grip, and the man sighed, then Tony stared at him, awaiting a response.

"I... I think they were with a few groupies who were in here the other night. I remember, because the band they're traveling with performed a couple of numbers upstairs, and this brunette..." He pointed at Davina, "She was out of her head drunk. I had to get one of my guys to throw her ass out."

This was music to Tony's ears, "Do you happen to know the name of this band, and where their next show be at?"

The man took a second to regain his composure before replying, "I've got a flier of theirs around here somewhere, it's got all the dates and venues if I recall." the man replied, and began to search his desk, until he found an old, crumpled sheet of paper, with the band's logo of a cartoon female Devil printed on it.

"Here you go, you can have that - not my bag. They're like Zeppelin you know, if Zeppelin had been shit." the man added, then handed Tony the flier.

"What's this? Nine p.m. tomorrow night at the Matador Inn?"

"Oh, that's that new place that's opened, pretty small potatoes, but seems popular with the younger crowd."

Tony glanced to Christopher then looked at the man one final time, "Thank you, pops, you've been very helpful." He said.

CHAPTER 18

(Los Angeles)

A knock came to a door of an upstairs office at Donnelly's Night Club. Marcus stood by a large screen TV. It was showing behind the scenes of a photo shoot, where two naked girls were posing beside a swimming pool as a photographer took pictures. The knock repeated, and he switched the screen off then walked back to his desk.

"Come in..." He responded.

The door opened, where a full-length poster was displayed showing Justine dressed in a school uniform and holding a big round lollipop. Malcolm then entered, looking serious.

"Hey there, Malcolm, what can I do you for?" Marcus asked, sitting on the edge of the desk.

"Nothing in particular, I was just you know, wonderin' if you'd heard anything new regarding Gerard Jones."

Marcus sighed, "I understand how you feel, Malcolm, believe me, but haven't you ever considered that all this could just be coincidence?"

"I wish it was, but let's look at the facts..." Malcolm replied, coming to stand in front of Marcus, "The keys to my lock up went missing just after my dear sister paid me a visit, then when I went to the lock up, my Porsche had been stolen and that black van of Gerard's was parked, seemingly abandoned outside. Add to all this Cameron deciding to vanish, maybe even run away with her girlfriend, and at the same time, our good friend Gerard Jones decides to do a disappearing act."

"Do you want a drink? You look like you want a drink." Marcus asked.

"No, thanks."

"Alright. Well, since we last talked, I've had a few guys stake out some of Gerard's old haunts, and also had one or two of his friends kept an eye on."

"Well, that's good I suppose."

"But wouldn't it be easier to just inform the Police about the stolen Porsche? My people can work fast, but the Cops, they have the advantage in numbers."

"No, that isn't an option." Malcolm said, walking over to the TV and glancing at its blank screen, himself and the office reflected back "Cameron wouldn't run away for no reason, Marcus. She's in trouble, and if Gerard is involved, bringing the Cops in could easily endanger her life."

Marcus stepped into view as Malcolm remained looking at the screen, "I've got my best people on it, Malcolm. We'll find him, and your sister, I am sure of it." He added, but Malcolm failed to reflect his confidence.

(Las Vegas)

As evening drew in, Davina was seated on the back seat of the band's tour bus with Andrew, the two of them sharing some pot beyond a series of seats. As she exhaled smoke, Andrew put his arm around her, and squeezed her against him.

"Tonight's gonna rock - you planning on sticking around for the show?" He asked.

"Wouldn't miss it for the world." She replied, taking another, lingering drag.

Then a noise was heard, and Andrew looked down the length of the bus, as Johnny and Cameron entered.

"Hey, you guys gonna sit there getting high all night, or you gonna get ready?" Johnny asked, wearing a long fur coat with a thick, bushy collar, and Cameron stared over his shoulder, wearing a gold coloured, silk shirt and black, flared trousers.

"We're just finishing up, mate, then we'll be right with you..." Andrew replied feeling more than a little stoned.

Davina exchanged eye contact with Cameron, who looked at her with as expected, disapproval, then her and Johnny exited the bus, leaving them alone.

She sat forward as she took another drag of the joint, then passed it back to Andrew.

"Can I tell you something, Andy?" She then said.

"Sure, baby cakes."

"Have you ever done or said something you not felt entirely proud of? By that I don't mean stealin' out of your Momma's purse or swearing at your high school teacher - I mean, something really bad, that no matter which way you look at it, ain't ever gonna fix itself..."

"What's brought this on, babe?" Andrew quizzed, stroking Davina's hair from behind.

"Maybe it's the Pot, but, I dunno, I was just thinkin'..."

"Well, I suppose - haven't we all? I was married a few years back, to this Asian girl I met on the road, hot little firecracker who could go like the clappers. But you know how it goes, after a while, I could see things were not going to work. So I shot through, didn't leave a note or nothing ... I guess that's something I'm not exactly proud of."

Davina nodded, suddenly feeling very honest, "I only wish mine had been that clichéd."

Andrew smirked, "Why? What's a girl like you got to feel bad about?"

"Well, after I got into the drugs scene, I was

scared Cam... I mean, Selina was going to leave me. She's never liked me doing Heroin or any of that shit, and it caused some arguments between us, because I could never seriously consider giving it up. My life was complicated enough back then without having to handle things in a state of full consciousness. You get me?"

"Yeah babe, I know that feeling." Andrew said, taking a drag of the pot then breathing a cloud of smoke into the air and coughing.

Davina squirmed, "Hey, I don't know if I should go into this. I mean, I feel guilty, but is confessing my shit to you gonna make like I never did any of it? Perhaps in a few year's time, I'll look back on this and laugh, who knows?"

Andrew glanced to her, "Well, I really wouldn't beat yourself up about it, whatever it is, babe - time is a wonderful healer."

Davina smiled, "Yeah, I hope so."

Andrew then sat up beside her, "We better go and get ready." He said.

"In a minute. Let me finish that, yeah?" Davina sighed, and Andrew took the joint from between his lips and handed it to her.

*

As it turned nine o'clock, the band were getting ready back stage at the evening's booked venue:

The Matador Inn, and Cameron stood by the closed curtains that concealed the stage from a loud, boisterous crowd.

"There's a lot of people out there tonight." She said to a red-haired girl she knew as 'Penelope'.

Cameron took a peek at the populated bar beyond the stage, and her heart raced with anticipation. Then Penelope looked with her.

"It's not that many - in Cleveland there was over fifteen hundred, and this one time in New York, you couldn't see to the end of the concert hall for all the waving hands 'n' jumping bodies."

Cameron looked at her admiringly, "You been on the road a long time then?" She asked.

"Since I was sixteen. Most of the girls were young when they got into Johnny's lyrics. They're timeless."

Cameron smiled, guessing Penelope was probably older than she looked, maybe even in her thirties. It was a very attractive lifestyle she led, and as Cameron looked towards a corridor leading off to individual dressing rooms, she realised that Davina, standing talking to one of the other girls, was already smitten.

Leaving Penelope to ponder the imminence of the gig, Cameron walked towards Davina, then paused as Andrew appeared and planted a kiss on her friend's lips. He was dressed in skin-tight leather trousers and a bright pink frilly shirt. At that moment, she hated Andrew, even though she hardly knew him, yet he was distracting Davina from her, and that was churning Cameron up inside.

Waiting until they left her view, Cameron stepped down from the stage and entered the corridor, then stopped at Johnny's dressing room. She tried the handle, and the door opened. She poked her head in, then gasped on seeing Johnny slouched in a chair being sucked off by the Black girl with the afro she knew as 'Sandy', who was knelt between his legs.

Over loud speaker, a man's voice was then heard:

"This is the Matador Inn. Welcome one and all! Tonight, for your entertainment and listening pleasure, we are proud to present, all the way from Liverpool, England - the Rock-tastic Little Devils!!!"

Johnny reacted to the announcement, and Cameron quickly moved from the door, leaving it ajar. Then as she walked away, she looked from one corridor to the next, seeing Johnny, Andrew and several other band members all fastening their clothing as they left their dressing rooms. She couldn't help but snigger as they headed for the stage. Damn, they must have thought they were Aerosmith.

CHAPTER 19

Sandy, the Black girl Cameron had discovered in Johnny's dressing room, stepped out from the Exit at the rear of the Matador Inn to be met by a big, muscular doorman.

"What, you not checking out the band, Sinoiress?" He asked in a Mexican accent

"Maybe in a moment. Just needed some air." She replied, carrying a can of sprite.

The doorman eyed her up and down, smiling, "Haven't I seen you here before?"

"I don't think so. The band has only come back to the states in the last two weeks, and we've only been in Vegas a couple of days."

"Really? So do you like it here?" the doorman asked.

"Mmm, yeah it's OK. You know the more places we go, the more people we seem to pick up. Just traveling through Palm Springs last week, we came upon these two girls who looked like they'd run away from home. We have a knack for attracting fuckin' losers it seems."

Then the sound of approaching voices and laughter alerted them, and they looked towards the rear car park, just as two men appeared from the shadows, one carrying boxes stacked one on top of the other.

"Hold up, who are these banditos?" the doorman remarked.

As the two men grew nearer, their conversation could be made out.

"So what's in these boxes?" asked Christopher.

"Cake, Beer - probably for the after show party." Tony replied, then they reached the door.

"Hang on fellas, what's this? I ain't been told 'bout no delivery."

Tony glanced to Christopher, who then let the boxes slip from his hands.

"Fuck!" He cursed as they fell to the ground, spilling confectionery all over as the doorman rushed to help.

"Hey, let me give you a hand." He said.

Suddenly, a gun was pressed to his head. BANG!! Sandy fell against the doorframe, mouth a scream on her lips, but nothing was heard as Christopher held a smoking 9mm. The doorman hit the floor face down, blood quickly spreading out around him.

In the corridor beyond the door, the fat, ageing

female owner descended a flight of stairs, and loud rock music could be heard close by. A second gunshot then rang out, and she stopped in her tracks. The music ended, a crowd cheered, then the woman felt a breeze and heard the squeak of hinges. She looked down the corridor, then a third gunshot pierced the air, and she dropped to the floor, a hand clutched to her breast.

On the stage, Johnny looked back to his bass player, who shrugged his shoulders.

"Relax man, this is Vegas!" the lead guitarist then shouted, and began to strum the cords, as Johnny looked back to the puzzled crowd, and re-approached the Mic.

"Probably somebody who hasn't paid their taxes! This one's called 'White Dove'." He said, his voice echoing out across the audience, who then cheered and whistled encouragement.

By the bar, Cameron sat watching the band as she drank from a bottle of Smirnoff.

"You with this motley crew, honey?" a Hawaiian barman asked.

Cameron nodded back at him, and took another swig. She sighed heavily, lips soaked with liquor.

"You should go steady on that stuff, the night's still young." the barman remarked, cleaning a glass with a towel.

Cameron watched Johnny sing the band's

signature ballad, but felt out of place to the family that surrounded him on the road and at gigs. She didn't belong, and neither did Davina.

"It's all the same though, isn't it? Another city, another town, nothing changes."

The barman listened quietly, sensing Cameron had something to get off her chest.

"But who am I kidding? This isn't me. Never has been. I'm just pretending to be Penny Lane and blocking out who I really am."

"Penny Lane?" the Barman asked.

Cameron smirked, taking another swig then replied, "Forget it. It's the Vodka. Maybe I should find a room and lie down for a while."

In the corridor, Tony walked, stepping over the body of the female owner, then opened his long trench coat to reveal a pump-action shotgun. He left bloody footprints on the carpet as he proceeded, turning down the next corridor and continuing towards the music.

Inside one dressing room meanwhile, Davina was slumped over a table. An empty glass was in her hand, and saliva had formed a small puddle next to her head. Suddenly a loud gunshot made her jolt awake, and she looked up, vision blurred as she stared at the door. Then the handle began to rattle, and she sat up quickly as the door clicked open.

Outside in the corridor, Penelope lay against a wall, her voice box having been blown out at close range, and she choked, coughing up a gallon of blood. In front of her stood Christopher, his 9mm pistol held by his side as he pushed the dressing room door inwards.

On the stage, Johnny was reaching the crescendo of the song's chorus, and his lead guitarist was going crazy at his side. Just then Tony entered stage right - and the music died.

Cameron gulped the last of her Smirnoff, then gasped to see the big, trench-coat wearing Italian standing just feet from where Johnny held pride of place. Johnny glanced to him, then looked alarmed as he saw the shotgun.

"What is this?" He said, voice echoing through the microphone.

Tony then pumped the chamber of the shotgun, and fired. The crowd screamed, and Johnny involuntarily stage dived, landing on top of some of the crowd as a result. Cameron quickly got down from the stool she had been sitting on, and looked around in panic. Tony approached the mic and grinned. The crowd gradually quieted.

"Viiivaaaa Las Vegas!!" He then announced, "You know, I've always wanted to say that!"

In the dressing room, Davina backed off to the wall as Christopher approached.

"Davina, isn't it?" He asked, "You don't look half as pretty in real life."

Davina looked genuinely scared, "Who the fuck!?" She quizzed.

"Elvis Presley at your service. Who was you expecting?" Christopher replied.

"Is this about the money? Because if it is, we can just give it you right back, that ain't no problem."

Christopher smirked, "This is no longer about the fuckin' money, sweetheart, this is about respect … and you and your friend seem to be lacking a whole lot it."

Davina stared at him. He was a lot bigger than her.

"Hey, call this a fair fight? I ain't even packin'." She said.

"Huh, I guess not. Alright babe, forget the guns, lets me and you go, right here, one on one." Christopher replied, and replaced his 9mm in the holster inside his jacket.

Cameron made her way through the crowd, pushing people out of the way in her urgency to escape.

"So tell me, how many of you seen a dead body, other than tonight?" Tony's voice continued over loud speaker.

The crowd was dumb struck and frozen in fear, whilst the other members of the band kept their distance.

"Not that many, I'm willing to bet. I haven't really been here before. My friends say it's the gamblin' capital of the world and all that, but you know, once you've played the odd roulette table, lost a couple of grand at black jack, the place for me at least, kinda loses its edge."

Cameron hurried on, then paused as she saw three similar Italian men enter the bar by the entrance doors, and suddenly she dropped to the ground, continuing on hands and knees.

Davina was thrown against the wall of the corridor, leaving a smear of blood as she slid drunkenly forward, then stumbled and fell to her knees. Christopher walked out of the dressing room nursing a grazed fist, and proceeded to kick Davina until she collapsed flat on her face, close to where Penelope now lay dead.

"How many times you done this?" She breathed, then raised herself up on her arms, struggling to get to her feet.

"You talk too much!" Christopher then replied, grabbing her by the hair, then slammed her face into the other wall.

Davina grunted on impact, then turned, stumbling backwards, and created a small distance between Christopher and herself. Her mouth was awash with blood, and she was sure she'd swallowed a tooth.

"I bet you think you're so fuckin' tough, huh?

Get off beatin' the crap out of defenceless young women do ya? That the only way you can get hard?" She asked, backing away still further, the corridor that led to the stage now visible.

"Do you know what? I expected more." Christopher remarked, "I heard you were tough, had some guts. But it's true what they say, isn't it? Reality really is stranger than fiction." He then revealed a switchblade.

Davina took one look at the huge, shining blade, then her eyes grew stern. Without further hesitation, she ran at him, like all logic and rational thought had just flown out the window, and she grabbed him around the neck, forcing him back on himself until he hit a door near the entrance to the next corridor, and it swung open, causing him to fall down a flight of steps. Davina reached out instinctively and grabbed the railings, preventing herself from following, as he tumbled down the hard stone steps, and an unmistakable snap sound was heard as he hit the floor below.

Davina panted for breath, then crawled back into the corridor, and stood up. At first she didn't notice the switchblade imbedded in her side. She took a few seconds to catch her breath, then walked slowly forward, before pausing as she felt a cold sensation. She applied her hand to her waist, and then discovered the knife, and quickly pulled it out, looked at it, before discarding it to the floor and walking on. What had just happened didn't seem real to her. She was still feeling the effects of the alcohol mixing with the dope still dancing in her head, and as she proceeded back down the corridor, she felt light headed and confused.

Cameron scrambled to her feet, and looked nervously towards the stage, just as the bass player was thrown into the crowd behind her. People cried out and panic consumed each and every person, but as they began to move and shove one another, Tony fired a shot into the air, and silence was restored again.

"That's better. We don't want a fuckin' riot on our hands, do we?" He said into the microphone.

Then a crackling noise was heard, and he took out a CB radio, raising it to his mouth.

"Speak."

"We've got movement, boss - to your left." one of the Italians the other side of the crowd said, as he spotted Cameron edging towards a far door.

Tony looked over to her and his eyes widened, "Fuck! There! That's one of 'em!!" He cursed, then discarded the CB and rushed across the stage, just as Cameron looked at him, then made for the door.

The three other Italians suddenly pushed through the crowd, knocking people to the floor in their haste. Cameron entered a corridor and suddenly darted down it. She then skidded in a pool of blood as she reached the next corridor, and spotted

Penelope's body. Horrified, she was quick to hurry onwards.

On the stage, Tony reached a small set of steps and paused to pump the chamber of his shotgun again, when without warning, Andrew rugby-tackled him side on, and they both fell from the stage and hit the floor. The shot gun went off and the blast blew a girl's foot clean off as she stood just meters away, and she screamed, collapsing in agony as Andrew proceeded to wrestle the gun out of Tony's hands.

Soon, Cameron entered a corridor to discover the further sight of the female owner lying dead on the floor, then saw a weak-looking Davina resting against a wall.

"Davina! Shit..." Cameron gasped and rushed over to her friend, grabbing her with desperation.

"Hey baby - what took yah?" Davina replied with a dazed look in her eyes.

"Where were you? I couldn't see you in the bar - are you OK?"

"I'm just fine, baby..."

"God, you're high aren't you? What they do, someone hit you, Davina?" Cameron asked, seeing the blood that smeared Davina's face.

"I'm OK, honest ... and anyway, it's not all mine."

Cameron took hold of her friend's hand then

pulled her away from the wall.

"Let's get out of here then. I think we've outstayed our welcome in this town." She added, and the two of them hurried away.

Then as they neared the open Exit door, a gruesome blood-splattered Tony appeared some distance behind, and aimed his gun. Then just as he was about to fire, one of the other Italians collided with him, and the shotgun was knocked out of his hands.

"What you doing you fat fuck?!" He cursed as the big Italian looked puzzled.

"You see 'em boss? I'm sure that blonde chick came this way."

Tony shoved the Italian aside and stared down the corridor to see the Exit door swinging in the breeze, with no sign of Cameron or Davina.

*

A few minutes later, Cameron & Davina hurried down a narrow walk way, with Davina trailing behind.

"Can't we rest now, mommy?" Davina announced, somewhat drunk on the pain from a stab wound she didn't seem aware of, despite the blood that had already made its mark on the white blouse she was wearing.

"In a minute." Cameron replied, then they entered

a car park, to see a small Camper van all on its lonesome, not unlike the one Davina used to own.

"There!" She exclaimed, and ran over to it.

Suddenly she elbowed the window on the driver's side, shattering the glass, then reached in and opened the door. Davina hobbled around, as Cameron climbed in and reached across the passenger seat to unlock the other side.

"Right, if I just focus, I should be able to wire this baby up." She said as Davina slowly climbed inside and winced in agony as she contorted her body into a sitting position.

She watched breathlessly as Cameron snapped open the bottom of the steering wheel. Then having learnt everything from Davina, Cameron commenced a rather expert hot-wire job, until the Camper's engine roared into life.

"Good thing I paid attention these past few years - 'cause you're certainly in no fit state." Cameron commented, then adjusted the gear stick, and reversed out of the car park, swinging the van around to face the direction of the road, before applying the accelerator with a scream of burning rubber.

CHAPTER 20

(Los Angeles)

Early next morning, Mr Leone relaxed in the swimming pool at the rear of his house, sipping a raspberry cocktail through a straw, whilst two well-built Italian bodyguards stood nearby. A telephone rang out, and he picked up a cordless phone found floating on a miniature version of the inflatable lounger he reclined on.

"Leone speaking..." He said, then placed the cocktail on a wooden drinks tray as it floated past.

"Hey there, Boss - it's Tony."

"Tony my boy! Good news I hope?"

"I wish. We located the girls in Vegas, hanging out with some no-name band. We tried to grab them, but there were complications. Christopher's dead. I'm afraid we might have missed our only opportunity."

"Christopher's dead?" Mr Leone exclaimed, "This

really puts a dampener on my day. Was it one of the girls who did it?"

"It's hard to say. Looks like he fell down some stairs."

Mr Leone ran a hand over his face, "OK. Come home. We've let this thing drag on for long enough. It's time to call in 'The Scorpion'."

"You're calling in 'The Scorpion'?"

"That's what I said, isn't it?"

"Alright then. We'll be back home tonight, tomorrow at the latest, and er, sorry about all this, Boss."

"Don't worry about it, Tony; it's out of your hands now."

Mr Leone switched off the phone then looked to the house. Gerard Jones came limping out from the patio doors, aided by a walking stick, with the lower half of his leg in a steel brace.

"Who was that?" He asked, wearing a towelling robe.

Mr Leone just offered an expression of disdain.

(9:30a.m.)

The camper van sat in a large car park outside LAX international airport, and the curtains were drawn across the windows. A strong sun beat down on it, with people walking by, oblivious to its occupants.

In the driver's seat, Cameron slowly opened her eyes and squinted at the harsh daylight peeking in at her. For a second she had to recollect where she was, then images from the previous night flashed in her head and she let out a groan. Her body ached from falling asleep from exhaustion in such an uncomfortable position, too nervous to crash out in the back like Davina had done. She rubbed her crusty eyes, then yawned loudly.

"Davina? You awake? What time is it baby?" She called to her friend.

No reply came. Slowly Cameron sat forward, glancing at the analogue display on the dash – but it had stopped reading the correct time long ago, so she guessed it wasn't really three o'clock in the afternoon. She looked to the door, a cooling breeze coming in from the broken window immediately soothing. She smiled to herself – at least the worst was over.

She climbed into the back to see the shape of Davina curled up under a moth-eaten blanket, just one foot peeking out.

"Hey wake up sleepy head." She said, and then crawled to the side, sitting on her haunches and prodded the shape gently. Nothing.

"Damn girl, you must have been stoned … time to wake up now, we need to make tracks." She added.

Cameron frowned. She realised she couldn't even hear breathing, in fact nothing at all. In an instant, a terrible feeling appeared in her belly. She slowly reached up to the hem of the blanket covering Davina's head, yet hesitated from pulling it away.

"Davina?" Cameron whispered nervously, then with one quick movement - she tore the blanket back to reveal...

Cameron fell against the wall of the van. Her mouth was open, then she turned away, almost hugging the wall as if begging for someone to hold her and tell her it was alright. After a moment, she turned her head and cast her eyes again on her friend and lover, now lying in a thick pool of her own blood. Davina had bled out through the night, and going by her colour-less complexion, she had been dead for several hours.

"No..." Cameron gasped in disbelief, "Please God no..."

Then as people walk past the van, a cry of despair was heard, and they stopped to look. Inside, Cameron panted and quickly moved away from Davina, feeling desperate, whilst at the same time considerably scared. She then noticed blood staining her trousers.

She looked to a small wardrobe, and opened the double doors to discover a variety of shirts and a suitcase. Wasting no time, she reached down to the case and opened it, revealing an untidy assortment, more than likely belonging to a man.

Finding a leather wallet and opening it, she thumbed through some ten and twenty dollar bills, but little else. She placed the wallet to one side, next to Davina's feet, then picked out a pair of striped, old fashioned trousers. They were definitely not her taste, but considering the blood stains on her own trousers, she was in little position to be choosey.

Eventually Cameron climbed out of the camper van, and looked around as strangers walked by and cars whizzed past on the road behind. She closed the van door silently, almost as if she was scared of waking Davina, then slowly proceeded towards the airport building.

As she walked, she opened a purse she owned which had a Velcro fastening, and looked at a picture within, of Malcolm, Patricia & herself, taken some years ago when she was still a kid. It was the only thing she had managed to retain in the chaos of recent events, due mainly to her never going anywhere without it.

Retrieving a small key, she stared at it as she replaced the purse in the back pocket of her new trousers, then stopped, giving a deep sigh of dismay as a tears lingered in her eyes. She glanced back to the van, now some distance behind, and it looked so lonely, all on its own with no other vehicles near it. She felt guilty for abandoning Davina like she had, but what choice did she have?

She was still on dangerous ground - that much hadn't changed, but perhaps now, even though it hurt her considerably to admit it, *things might be easier on her own.*

Cameron entered the airport minutes later, and walked through a heavily populated lounge area until she reached a long row of personal lockers. She scanned the numbers carefully, then inserted the small key in one, and opened it to reveal the large, bulging hold-all. She looked around nervously before grabbing it, and then marched back through the lounge towards one of the terminals.

She paused to scan the flight times lit up on a digital display high above, and saw that a plane destined for Washington D.C. and another for Florida had just arrived, and boarding was in an hour. She saw people cueing at a check out, and thought long and hard. How easy would it be to just disappear? After all, that had pretty much been the plan between Davina and herself all along. But deep down, she knew she had only intended to keep running for so long. Once Davina's time was up the rest of the journey was a question mark. Cameron hadn't planned that far ahead. Now though, Davina was already dead, and to continue on without her seemed unthinkable. It had all been for her, Cameron had risked everything for the woman she loved.

Feeling close to sobbing, she turned away and headed back towards the entrance doors. She returned to the car park crying, and increased her pace as the hold-all grew heavier and heavier the more she carried it. Taking a different route out of the car park than the one she had initially drove in by, she proceeded down the street and turned the corner. Then she stopped, overcome with emotion, and the tears were streaming down her face. She sat down on a low wall and tried to catch her breath.

As seconds turned into minutes, she gradually calmed herself, and dried her eyes on her sleeve. Then a presence alerted her, and she jolted, looking to see a scruffy, bearded homeless man, who seemed to appear out of nowhere.

"Hey, buzz off, will yah?" She snapped.

"Sorry Miss - you couldn't spare some change, could you? I haven't eaten in days." He replied, stinking of alcohol and God knows what else.

Cameron stared at him sternly, then stood up, glancing down at the hold-all. She looked at the tramp again, then began to walk on, but stopped, glancing back to find he was still focused on her. She sighed then handed him the hold-all.

"Here … knock yourself out." She said, and walked away, feeling like the heaviest weight had been lifted from her shoulders.

The homeless man stared at the hold all, puzzled. He then sat down on the wall and placed the canvas sack between his feet, before slowly running the zip from one end to the other. It sprung open, and his face lit up, as he found it to be filled to bursting with more money than he had seen in his entire life.

"Oh, jeez!" He exclaimed, and looked down the street for Cameron, but it was too late ... she was gone.

CHAPTER 21

Patricia Willis walked through a department store with Barbara, looking at designer clothing as gentle music played.

"I'm sure that would look very nice." Barbara said, referring to a black trouser suit.

Patricia smiled and nodded, but such attire just brought back memories of her Private Detective years, which still made her feel uneasy. They had come out for a bit of retail therapy, which had always worked in the past, but for numerous reasons, wasn't having the desired effect this time. Patricia just felt bored, her mind wondering to repetitive thoughts, more often than not concerning her sister.

A melody was then heard, and she took her cell out of her bag, noticing to her surprise her younger sister's name.

"Hello?"

"Patricia? I can't talk long - are you alone?"

Patricia looked shocked, at first unable to reply.

"Is Mom or Dad there? If they are, don't say a word; just go out of the room or something."

She responded to her sister's voice like it was part of her. She moved away and their mother continued to browse, oblivious.

"Cameron?" She whispered.

"That's right. I'm coming home, but I really need to contact Malcolm first."

"Fuckin' hell Cam', do you have any idea how worried we've been?"

"Yeah, I know sis, and I'm sorry, I truly am. You need to understand though, I really had no choice. I'm ok though, at least for now. I've called you 'cause they're less likely to be watching you. Do you think you can get a message to Malcolm?"

Patricia felt flummoxed, "What do you mean? Who are 'they'? You're in trouble, aren't you?"

"I'll explain it all to you someday, Patricia, but for now I have to be brief - just tell big bro I'll be at the Hotel later this afternoon. And tell him that a little bit of all of this kind of concerns his new business partner."

"What's that supposed to mean? You're not making sense." Patricia said, then the line went dead, "Cam... CAM!" - Patricia lowered the cell, puzzled but also relieved.

Cameron's words then ran through her mind as recent events were recalled. Patricia stood in an office, shaking hands with Marcus Donnelly, looking somewhat nervous.

'...a little bit of all of this kind of concerns his new business partner...'

"God dammit." She breathed with dread.

*

Patricia returned home with Barbara, and hurried upstairs as soon as they entered the door.

"Patricia! Aren't you going to take your bags?" Barbara exclaimed, dropping a load of designer-labelled shopping bags on the floor.

"Later, Mom - I've just got something I need to do." Patricia called back.

Patricia entered her room and removed a brand new suede jacket, tossing it on the bed, and then applied her cell phone to her ear.

"Pick up...pick up..." She said impatiently.

"Heeere's Johnny!! The person you're trying to reach is unavailable at the moment. Leave your message after the tone. Thanks." came Jack Nicholson's voice.

Patricia sighed, lowering the cell, and hurriedly began to type out a text message instead.

* *

Later that afternoon, Malcolm entered an elevator at the Hotel with Jeanie, and took his cell phone from inside his suit jacket.

"Who you calling?" Jeanie asked.

"Nobody - just checking my messages." Malcolm replied, then switched his cell on, pressing the buttons repeatedly.

"Marcus wants me to go and supervise at Tombstone tomorrow night - apparently they've got some big Country & Western singer doing a gig there, and he's expecting quite a turn out."

"Country, huh? Maybe I should come along. It might be fun." Jeanie added.

"Maybe." Malcolm replied.

Leaving the elevator and proceeding down the corridor, they passed a well-dressed porter pushing a trolley of laundry. On reaching the door, Jeanie took out a set of keys and inserted one in the lock, then gasped to find the door already open. Malcolm lowered his phone, frowning with concern.

"We been broken into?" He asked, and Jeanie backed off.

Malcolm then went to pocket his phone, but hesitated when he read Patricia's name.

"Hang on..." He said, and Jeanie looked sternly at him.

"What is it?" She asked.

He selected the message and read it. Jeanie waited for an answer.

"Well?" She urged.

"Cameron's back." Malcolm announced, and pushed the door of the Hotel room open, walking inside.

"Come out, Cameron!" He exclaimed, entering the living room to the sound of a television programme, then he paused as he recognised his kid-sister sitting in the armchair, her feet propped up on a coffee table.

"Hey there bro - how's it hanging?" She said with an innocent-looking smile, still wearing the clothes of whoever the owner of that camper van was.

Malcolm sighed, putting his phone away, then glanced back to Jeanie, who lingered in the doorway.

"You'd better make us two coffee's." He said to her.

Jeanie left, leaving Malcolm to look back at Cameron, relieved but angry at the same time.

Soon, Cameron drank the last of her coffee, whilst Malcolm sat on the sofa, staring her out. In the kitchen, Jeanie was drying some dishes and casually eves-dropped.

"Alright. Now let's hear it." She heard Malcolm demand.

"What do you want to know?" Cameron replied, leaning forward to place her empty mug on the coffee table.

"What made you up sticks and leave? I suppose you think you're real smart to lift my keys and steel the Porsche from the lock up."

"I was desperate, bro. And before you ask, no, I haven't brought your beloved car back - we had to dump it. It's not like you haven't got a dozen more."

"We?" Malcolm remarked.

"OK, it was like this. Now don't go crazy or anything or I'll leave right now. I was seeing Davina."

"Davina? You told me she was in prison."

Jeanie couldn't help but gasp, all too familiar with the stories of what that girl had done to the family.

"I lied, ok? You, Mom, Dad, even Patricia couldn't handle what I really was, that I could be interested in girls. So it was easier for us if you guys didn't know anything. But well you see, Davina had got into drugs a while back, and she told me, about six months ago that she had been diagnosed with some terminal illness. She was suffering Malcolm, and all I could do was watch."

"Hang on, are you telling me Davina was dying?"

"Yes. It was horrible. The drugs were the only thing

that seemed to make her feel better. She became reliant on them, and the stuff the clinic gave her was no alternative."

"Who was she getting these drugs from?" Malcolm asked.

"Well, you're not gonna like this, but her dealer was none other than that scumbag, Gerard Jones."

"Oh... that figures. I knew he was involved in this."

"But Davina ended up owing him, and she couldn't pay, so Gerard had her beaten up and put in hospital. After that she couldn't turn to him anymore, and tried to make me get hold of some stuff for her. Now I didn't want to go begging for that shit off Gerard Jones, so I got some friends together, and tried to turn over a Pharmacy - the same one I got arrested for."

"Jesus Christ, Cameron - you did something like that, for her?"

"I couldn't handle seeing Davina the way she was. To be quite honest there was probably nothing I wouldn't have done for her. You don't have to understand. So after that job went the way it did, I felt I had no alternative but to turn to Gerard."

"You should have come to me. We could have worked something out." Malcolm said.

"Like what? Would you have risked everything you have, with Jeanie, just to get drugs for somebody you despise?? Don't bullshit me, Malcolm - you would have laughed in my face!"

Malcolm couldn't help but agree.

"So, what happened when you turned to Gerard?"

"Well, I got the drugs for Davina, but things didn't work out. Gerard became possessive, and wanted me to do things with him, sexual things."

"That mother-fucker. I'll fucking kill him!" Malcolm cursed, looking away for a brief second, picturing Gerard's smug grin.

Jeanie was pouring herself a coffee, stirring the cream with a spoon. She had always feared something like this. She liked Cameron but knew she always attracted trouble, and now she was dragging Malcolm into her latest escapade. This wasn't good.

"And well, I went along with it, just to help Davina. But after a while it became a problem. He used to hit me, made like it was just a bit of fun - being a bit rough turned him on. Then I overheard a conversation one evening, and suddenly I realised a way out of the whole mess."

Malcolm got up, walking across the room, and poured himself a Brandy from a drinks cabinet, struggling to contain his anger.

"What conversation?" He asked.

"I heard everything when you showed up after Gerard handed fake money over to Marcus Donnelly. Shit Malcolm, even I've heard of that thug."

"What?? What do you mean? You were there?" Malcolm gasped, then recalled the mattress in the apartment living room, and the handcuffs he had picked up. He began to feel nauseous.

"I was in the bathroom." Cameron continued, "I heard it all. Then while I was getting dressed in Gerard's bedroom, I found a map. I tell you now, it was like something straight out of a cowboy movie."

Malcolm poured the brandy into a glass, then drank it down in one gulp, before pouring another. In the background, Jeanie appeared in the doorway between the main room and the kitchen, steaming mug of coffee in hand.

"So I copied the map onto a piece of paper, and after hearing what I heard, I put two and two together, figuring that Gerard had ripped Marcus Donnelly off big time, and I had just discovered the answer to mine and Davina's prayers."

"What happened then?"

"I told Davina my theory, and together, we went to the location on the map, a cemetery in East LA. There we found a grave, and dug it up."

"… so that's where the prick was keeping the cash. It all makes sense now." Malcolm remarked.

"Yeah, and so before Gerard had time to discover we'd lifted the money, Davina and I were gonna run away, and I was planning on making whatever time she had left, the best it could possibly be."

"But? There's always a 'But'." Malcolm added.

"But somehow, Gerard found out, and he nearly killed both of us. But Davina got the better of him, and we had to make a run for it with no time to grab our packed bags or even leave a letter of goodbye."

Malcolm swallowed the second Brandy and walked back to the sofa, sitting down.

"So I presume Gerard came after you?" He asked calmly.

"I don't know, but he must have, because these guys caught up with me and Davina in Vegas, where we were hanging out with a band traveling from gig to gig."

"What guys?"

"I don't know, things happened kind of fast. I don't even think they were after the money - it was like they just wanted us dead."

"Oh God, Cameron. Didn't you realise that even if Davina was involved, I would still have done everything I could to help you??"

"By the time that even crossed my mind, it was too late. I'm only here now because I'm scared Gerard will send someone after me, otherwise I'd never stop running."

"Why too late? What happened?"

"We thought we'd got away. Me and Davina managed to escape from these psychos - and stole a van to make our getaway. We were all set to grab the money and move on - but when I woke up next morning ..."

Cameron paused as she painfully recalled that horrible moment of discovery.

"What?"

"Davina was dead." She said quietly.

"You mean, she died from her illness?"

"No. She had been cut or something. She bled out during the night, while I just slept like a baby."

She sighed and bowed her head, placing one hand over her eyes. Malcolm moved closer and touched her arm. For a few moments they sat in silence, the glow from the muted TV lighting them both up.

"So, Cameron, I realise this has been tough for you. But you need to tell me ... where's the money?" Malcolm eventually asked.

"It's gone!" She snapped, then lowered her hand, eyes streaming, "I gave it away, alright?"

Malcolm looked stunned, "You did what??"

Cameron stared at him.

"So what? It meant nothing anymore - what did I want with all that money now Davina was gone? I only took it because of her - I risked everything because I loved her, and now she is dead!!"

Cameron got up and walked over to the fireplace, where a mirror was hung. She looked at herself with disgust, then turned back to Malcolm, wiping her eyes on her shirt sleeve. She looked to Jeanie for a second who remained silent, but her face was a picture of sympathy. Then a ringing was heard, and Malcolm got up, taking his cell out and raised it to his ear.

"Marcus?" He said.

Cameron looked at him with anticipation.

In a car meanwhile, Marcus drove whilst speaking into a phone of his own, "Malcolm? It's Marcus - I've got big news for you buddy." He said.

"Oh yeah?" Malcolm replied and Cameron stepped forward, "Funny you should call - I was just thinking of calling you."

"Well you're gonna want to hear this, Malcolm." Marcus continued, "Gerard Jones has just been spotted. It looks like he's been staking out your parents place most of the day. Maybe that hunch you had about him and your little sister was right, and he's now waiting for her to make an appearance. I'm on my way over to you now. It's time we got to the bottom of this."

Malcolm looked to Cameron sternly, realising events were about to get real.

"Alright. I'll see you in a minute, Marcus." He agreed, then ended the call.

Cameron stared at Malcolm with bated breath.

"What did he want?" She asked.

"Seems your friend Gerard is back in town also."

CHAPTER 22

Showdown in Los Angeles

Malcolm walked across the large car park at the front of the Hotel, as it began to get dark. Parked by the road was a grey-metallic Jaguar XKR, and the headlights were on full beam.

"Come on, get in." Marcus said as Malcolm reached the car, then hurried around to the passenger side and climbed in.

Marcus adjusted the gears then applied the accelerator, and the sleek sports car sped off down the road.

As Marcus drove, the radio was on low, reporting on a recent news story:

'Tributes are still pouring in following last night's tragic events in Las Vegas. It has been confirmed that lead singer Jonny Richards of rock band The Little Devils, from Liverpool, England was shot dead on stage during a show at the popular Matador Inn. We'll keep with this story throughout the day as it develops.'

Malcolm produced a 9mm pistol from inside the jacket he was wearing, and checked the clip. Marcus switched off the radio as a song began to play.

"You really think you're going to need that?" Marcus remarked.

"Without a doubt. Let's just say I'm not exactly planning on shaking the guy's hand."

"I thought we were just going to beat a few answers outa him. Like firstly, where the fuck he's got your sister?"

Malcolm shook his head, "I don't need to worry about that no more - Cameron's safe and well, back at the hotel."

"What? When did this happen? Did she say where she's been all this time?" Marcus exclaimed.

"On the run from the exact same guy we're going after now. You see, he lied to you Marcus, he lied to both of us."

"I don't understand."

"He did steal your money and pay you off with counterfeit. Cameron got word of this, because the stupid girl was fuckin' him to get drugs for her Junkie girlfriend. But when she found out how he scammed us, she thought she'd scam him back, found out where the real cash was, and stole it right out from under his nose."

"And he found out. Now I get it. God this is bad. If we're going to do this Malcolm, we're gonna do it right - let me make a phone call, and get us some back up."

Malcolm looked at him, "Why do we need back up?"

"Why?" Marcus replied, lifting a telephone receiver from between the seats, "Because if someone like Gerard Jones has the balls the rip me off, then there has to be a third party involved. I'm taking no risks."

Malcolm watched Marcus press the buttons on the receiver and hold it to his ear, his other hand gripping the wheel.

Back at the Hotel, a tall, bearded man dressed in a long, black leather coat with a black polo-neck jumper underneath, entered the foyer and approached the desk. A young male Porter was sat reading Playboy.

"Sorry to disturb you, friend, I was wondering if you could help me?" He said, well-spoken and his face reflected a wise nature - he looked to be in his late fifties.

"Of course, Sir, what's the problem?" the Porter replied, suddenly standing up and stuffing the magazine under the counter.

The man scanned his surroundings, spotting a

security camera high up in one corner.

In Malcolm's Hotel room, Cameron sat watching a re-run of Seinfeld, and laughed as she ate crackers out of a glass bowl on her lap.

"Do you want anything else to drink, Cameron?" Jeanie's voice called.

"No thanks, I'm fine for now - come and see this, it's funny." Cameron replied.

Jeanie walked back into the living room clutching a can of Diet Cola, and glanced to the TV screen.

"What is it?" She asked, leaning against the sofa where Cameron was situated.

"Dunno - but it's making me laugh, and I haven't done much of that in weeks. Almost thought I'd forgot how to."

Jeanie had never spent much time getting to know Malcolm's other sister, not like she had Patricia, but as she sat down on the sofa and cracked open her Cola, she realised that this was as good a time as any.

Just over an hour later, a gun-metal grey 4X4 Jeep arrived across the road from a set of tall gates belonging to the Willis mansion in Bel Air. Parked a short distance ahead of the jeep was a white BMW, and a light was on inside. In the Jeep, a Black guy applied a set of binoculars, and could just make out the back of the driver's head, hair black.

There wasn't another soul to be seen.

The Black guy then raised a CB radio and pressed a switch on the side.

"He's still here, Boss. Ready when you are." He whispered.

The line crackled, "Rock and roll..." a voice enthused.

The Black guy then glanced to a shot gun lying in the passenger seat, and suddenly switched his headlights back on and trod down on the accelerator.

The Jeep screeched to a halt beside the BMW and the Black guy pointed the shotgun out the window. Then he gasped to see a mannequin dummy in the driver's seat sporting a black wig, and as he looked around, the passenger side of the jeep opened and a gun went off, splattering the windscreen with blood and brain.

In Marcus' Jaguar meanwhile, Marcus yelled into a radio, "Bruno! What the fuck!?"

Malcolm stared at his friend with concern, then suddenly, bright light stung their eyes.

"Oh God!" He cursed, and Marcus dropped the radio, adjusted the gears and went to reverse out of the narrow alley they had parked in. But as he looked back, a car drove into view, blocking their exit.

"Jesus Christ - we're being ambushed!!" He exclaimed, stamping down on the breaks, and the Jag screeched to a halt inches from a black Limo that had appeared from nowhere.

The two of them looked ahead as the lights then faded to reveal three men in black suits, standing in front of two black cars, and packing some serious firepower.

"Oh fuck." Marcus said.

"Ok, don't panic!" Malcolm replied.

Marcus looked at him with an expression of absolute terror.

"You got a fuckin' plan then - because I'd sure like to hear it, Malcolm!"

Then the radio crackled, and they both looked down at it. Marcus picked it up and pressed the switch, but didn't say a word.

"Marcus, Marcus, Marcus - It's been a long time, hasn't it?" came a voice that Marcus suddenly found familiar.

"Mr Leone?" He announced.

Malcolm frowned, "Who the fuck is 'Mr Leone'??" He asked.

"Put Gerard on - I think this is all just a misunderstanding." Marcus continued.

"Sorry, Marcus - Gerard isn't here right now. Your nigger friend must have made a mistake, so we had to relieve him of his life."

Malcolm looked shocked, "If Gerard's not there, then where the fuck is ..."

Marcus looked at him, and his heart sank, "Oh no ... not again." He remarked, then looked back down the alley just as the men began to approach.

At the Hotel, Gerard entered the foyer, and glanced around to see the security camera sparking high up, and the bearded man sat behind the desk where the young Porter had once been.

"Took your time, didn't you, Mr Jones?" the man said, then stood up, adjusting his leather jacket before walking out from behind the desk.

"There's no hurry, Governor - Malcolm & Marcus needed time to get there, right? Now let's go to work. Ain't that how you people speak?"

The man smirked, then led the way as Gerard followed, revealing a Revolver from inside his coat.

Up in the Hotel room, Jeanie sat down on a bed in the master bedroom, and looked at a framed picture she held in her hand. It was of her and Malcolm, posing in front of the Eiffel Tower in Paris.

"What you lookin' at?" Cameron asked, standing in the doorway as soft music played in the background.

"Paris." Jeanie replied, and Cameron approached, sitting down next to Jeanie as she handed her the photo.

"Oh yeah - you got engaged there, right?" Cameron said.

Jeanie smiled, "Yeah - maybe we'll be married there someday also." She mused.

Cameron smiled at her, and looked at the photo again.

In the alley, Malcolm climbed out of the car, and raised his hands, "Gentlemen, surely we can come to some arrangement." He said.

Inside, Marcus fished out an UZI sub-machine gun from under the seat and chambered the first round.

"Get in here, Malcolm - you can't reason with these fucks!" He shouted.

Malcolm looked back to the Limo blocking their exit, then aimed his gun at the men not far in front.

"OK, you wanna play it like this? Then fuck you!" He cursed, and opened fire.

One man took a bullet in the shoulder, and he fell down, and as a result, a loud scream of gunfire erupted, and Malcolm dived back inside the car just as Marcus accelerated down the alley, propelling another man over the bonnet as they both ducked and the windscreen shattered. Then another man stepped out of the Limo and returned fire on the back of the car, piercing the bodywork, and Marcus let out a cry of adrenaline as he raced on, crashing through the two black cars, which forced the Jag into the air, where it turned over, then landed sliding on its roof in the street beyond.

After a brief silence, Malcolm crawled out from inside and slowly stood up in the glow of headlights. The tires of the car were still spinning. Then he was suddenly thrown back as gunfire ripped through the right side of his body, and he crashed to the ground, gasping for breath. The white BMW had arrived in the street in front of the overturned Jag, and the engine had been left running. Mr Leone then appeared, sporting a smoking AK47 and a cigar, grinning wickedly.

"End of the line, Marcus Donnelly - your rein over this town ceases tonight!" He exclaimed.

The other side of the Jag, Marcus stood up, his face bleeding from cuts to his jaw and the bridge of his nose.

"Hmm ... this is it then, huh?" He announced weakly, "I don't suppose we can settle all this with a smile and a hand shake??"

A short distance down the alley, one of the other men was still breathing, and nursing a gunshot to his shoulder. He looked up to see Marcus. He could also make out Mr Leone in the street beyond.

"Sorry Marcus - you know it doesn't work like that.

Whatever would Ol' Salvatore think if I was to turn soft now? I'm standing on a gold mine here, and I ain't screwing that up for nobody."

Then a gunshot rang out and Mr Leone jolted as a bullet hole appeared in the centre of his forehead. Marcus looked around in reaction, just as the surviving man ducked behind a car. Then Marcus walked out from the over-turned Jag to see a bloody Malcolm aiming a 9mm across the tarmac, smoke rising into the air. Mr Leone fell to his knees, before hitting the ground with a thud.

Marcus then looked back into the alley to see two further men appear, both armed. He aimed his UZI and opened fire, blowing them away in a heartbeat. The one hiding then scrambled to his feet and took cover in a doorway, hoping he hadn't been seen.

"Malcolm??" Marcus called as calm was restored, bullet casings littering the tarmac.

"What?" Malcolm replied, in agony.

"Stick with me buddy, I'll get you to a hospital."

"Fuck the hospital. Get me back to the Hotel!"

Marcus then walked alongside the car to see Malcolm slouched and was bleeding profusely, "Sorry, but you wouldn't survive the journey." He said.

"How are we going to get to the hospital then? The fuckin' car's totalled!"

Marcus then looked over to the BMW, "Relax man,

I've got reserves." He replied.

*

In the Hotel room, a squirming Jeanie lay face down on the sofa, with the bearded man sitting astride her, holding her hands behind her back and pressing a gun to her head. Her eyes were wide, but a strip of tape gagged her mouth. In the corner of the room, Gerard was securing Cameron to a dining chair with ropes, and she kicked and struggled furiously.

"You can't fight these odds, Cameron honey. Why you even tryin?" He said.

The man cocked the trigger back on his gun, increasing the pressure of the nozzle against Jeanie's head. Gerard then came and stood beside the sofa, and looked at Cameron with a child-like enthusiasm.

"Alright, she ain't going nowhere mate - what now?" He asked.

"Ask her about the money."

Gerard approached Cameron, "Now you gonna play nice if I take off the tape?" He asked.

She just stared at him silently, then he reached forward and tore the tape off, releasing a gasp.

"Now where is my money?" He asked.

"Fuck you!" She replied with hatred.

Gerard smirked, then suddenly swiped her across

her face. She winced in pain.

"You better tell me what I want to hear, sweet 'art, or Mr Serious 'ere is gonna end your friend."

From where Cameron sat, she could only see the back of the sofa, but Jeanie's dark hair was just visible peeking out from the arm.

"I don't have it anymore." She replied calmly.

Gerard frowned, "What do you mean you don't have it? Are you fuckin' jokin', because I've just gotta give the word, and your friend is history."

"Just like Davina, is that right - you murdering bastard!" Cameron then announced, and Jeanie's eyes bulged as if to say 'Cameron? What the hell are you doing?'.

"Come again?"

"You may not have done it yourself, but that makes no difference, you're still responsible!" Cameron continued.

Gerard smirked, glancing to the bearded man, known only as The Scorpion, who looked equally bewildered.

"Davina's dead then. Well, at least something good has come out of this mess." Gerard added.

"You fuckin' bastard! You didn't even know her!"

"Listen, I don't care about your fuckin' girlfriend - just tell me where the fuckin' money is you stupid bitch!!"

"I gave it away to some vagrant. I didn't want it

once Davina was gone, so I gave it to the first person I saw."

The Scorpion looked stunned, sitting back and relaxing his grip on the gun. Gerard stepped away, not taking his eyes off Cameron for one second.

"Forget this, man. I want to kill her. If she hasn't got the money, we no longer need her alive. Let's fuckin' kill both of them and get out of 'ere!" He said.

The Scorpion looked bemused, then a ringing was heard, and he took out a phone form an inside jacket.

"Hello?" He announced, "Salvatore!"

Gerard looked at him with concern. The Don, ringing directly?

"What, you can't get in touch with Leone?"

"What's he want?" Gerard whispered.

"The situation here? Well, the girl says she no longer has the money, apparently a friend she stole it for died, so she gave it away. I know, I know ... so, what do you want me to do about this?"

Gerard watched and listened, but was unable to hear what Salvatore was saying.

"OK, I understand, Salvatore - I'll sort it." The Scorpion said, then switched the phone off, putting it away.

"What did he say? Can we kill them?" Gerard asked eagerly.

"They're sending a car 'round - go out onto the balcony will you, and tell me when it arrives."

Gerard watched The Scorpion climb off Jeanie and ready his gun.

"Hey no - I want this - let me at least pop this one." He said, referring to Cameron with a wave of his revolver.

"This is what I do Mr Jones. You're not to kill anybody, The Don's orders. Now go and look out for the car."

Gerard sighed then limped awkwardly over to a set of closed drapes, and parted them to reveal some glass doors. As he opened them, releasing a cold breeze into the room, The Scorpion fixed a silencer to his gun, screwing it into place agonisingly slow. Cameron focused on him nervously, and Jeanie was close to tears, still lying on the sofa.

Then Gerard stepped out onto the balcony, and was treated to Venice Beach's stunning ocean view.

"Where'd he say the car would be?" He called back.

"On the road I presume." The Scorpion replied, stepping away from the sofa, then to Cameron's surprise, aimed his gun to the patio where Gerard's silhouette could be seen behind the drapes.

Cameron flinched as the trigger was pulled, and out on the balcony, a shocked Gerard staggered forward, collided with the wall, then tipped over the edge, plummeting 19 floors to his death.

Back in the room, Cameron stared in terror as

The Scorpion walked back towards the open living room door. Then much to her continued surprise, he just left, and a door was heard slamming shut seconds after.

She let out a sigh of relief, heart racing and looked to the sofa again. She struggled and tried to move across the room, nudging the chair an inch at a time, until she suddenly fell over, landing with a grunt. She then looked to the sofa as Jeanie sat up, removing the tape from her mouth, looking down at Cameron.

"You'd think he'd untie me."

"Don't push it, Cameron." Jeanie replied.

Many thanks for reading 'Showdown In Los Angeles'

I've always been very fond of this story, and have revised and polished it over several years. For me I like its straight forward thriller structure and with a focus on the character of Cameron Willis, I think it has a great feel, revolving around someone who isn't that tough, isn't always the best decision maker and a bit of a disaster. I think it makes her an enjoyable character to write. This novel also sets up much of the stories that follow and introduces characters and themes I go onto explore further in the remaining 3 books in my Dying Games Saga.

As for influences, looking back on this story I think I was heavily influenced by movies such as True Romance and to a smaller extent, Almost Famous. You might also notice many references to Westerns, of which this is kind of a modern-day take.

Ultimately, I hope you enjoyed the characters and situations I came up with and the novel as a whole wetted your appetite for more stories in this world, of which there is more to come.

Craig.

TO BE CONTINUED

Printed in Great Britain
by Amazon